RODS

A John Martin Story

by

James Warren McAllister

This book is dedicated to all who have touched my life and passed on too soon.

Table Of Contents

Prologue

1   1

2   15

3   29

4   48

5   69

6   87

7   103

Epilogue

About James W. McAllister

Other James W. McAllister Books

Prologue

My name is John Martin. I used to be a detective in the NYPD. It wasn't a bad job, really, as long as you don't mind long hours, low pay, no chance for a private life, and several people trying to kill you every day.

I became a cop so I could save the world, or so I thought. Investigating crimes seemed a way to make a real difference.

Then the strange things began to happen around me.

Now I investigate… other things.

Fantastic things seem drawn to me. I can't explain why they happen, or how they seem to find me, but they're real. This is the story of one of those strange things. Several strange, fantastic, and surreal things actually.

I'm recording this, because I hate typing, and because I wouldn't have enough time to type everything. Besides, there's nothing to type on in this cave. I may not have the time to finish, so I'll get right to it.

I'm in this dark hellhole trying to save my partner. And my wife. I think my plan will save us all. And everyone else.

If it doesn't, well… I'd better start at the beginning.

I'll never forget that first night…

It always happened in a stinking back alley. And in the middle of the night on my watch. Cold. Raining. Or hot and steamy. These things never happened in sunny flower studded meadows…

"Captain? Captain!"

"Yeah, Kawalski, isn't it? What do you have?"

"Double murders, Captain. The woman's over here."

Sergeant Kawalski pointed at the rusting green dumpster and began walking in that direction. I followed.

The stench and steam rose with equal enthusiasm into the cold April night. The mist mingled with Kawalski's breath and then mine when we reached the corner of the alley hidden by the dumpster.

"Caucasian female. Looks about 40. No make up, clothes are last year's style. No jacket. Purse is right there, unopened. Stabbed eight times. Two in her back, two in her face, the rest in her neck. M.E. said she's been dead about an hour."

I looked at the woman, then up and around the alley. The alley entrance was about fifty yards from us. A streetlamp flickered just out of view. The shadow of the medical examiner walked towards us carrying a large bag. From the shape of the shadow, Dr. Lisa Martin drew the short straw tonight.

Just my luck.

"Where's the other one?"

"He's right over here, Captain."

My eyes followed Kawalski's gesture. I saw a dark shape against the bricks near the basement hatch. I'd taken two steps towards it before the Medical Examiner's flashlight beam lit it up.

I almost puked.

"Damn, Lisa. Next time, warn a guy, will ya. What did this?"

"Best I can tell, somebody took most of him apart, a mouthful at a time. Not much left but bone."

If her voice had been any colder it'd be snowing. Was that for me, or from this scene?

Not that I'd blame her either way.

I looked back at the body. In places, the flesh was pared down to the bone. There was no skin left, and his eyes were gone. Hell, his face was gone down to the teeth. The blood splattered on the wall and along the ground formed a path back to the woman. Less blood than I would have thought, though. A big kitchen knife lay to the side about halfway between the bodies.

"What? Are you saying somebody *ate* this guy?"

"I'll need to run some tests to determine an official cause of death. But my first impression is that's what happened. Look at the bones, those scrapes." She didn't look up while she spoke.

I don't blame her for that, either.

I stepped back, pressing myself to the back of the alley. This didn't always work, but sometimes it did. I took a deep breath. I let it out and began scanning the entire area, starting at the street and sweeping back to my feet. I closed my eyes and took another deep breath.

I opened my eyes as I let this breath out slowly.

She was sobbing as she ran down the street. Panicked, terrified. Blood was running down her neck, thinned by the rain. She nearly fell when she turned into the

alley. He was close behind her, eyes wide,
knife held high. He caught up with her at the
dumpster. He grabbed her hair, pulled her
close. She went limp as he kissed her neck.
Five, ten, twenty seconds he held the kiss
before he pulled back. Twice the knife came
down into her neck before she turned. He kept
stabbing, twice more on her arm, twice on her
face, then twice on her chest. I could feel
the evil pouring out of him. It washed over
me as I watched the blood pour out of her.

He stood panting over her, bent over,
hands on his knees. His mouth was covered
with her blood. He licked the knife and his
lips clean. He stood up tall and smiled, the
meager light from the security lamp shining
off of his pale grey face. Then he jerked
back, as if he'd been hit. Blood fell from a
hole in his forehead. He jerked back again, a
second wound bleeding on his neck. He
screamed as a third, then a fourth wound
drove him back. Another strike, then another,
driving him back until he was against the
brick wall, sliding down, as chunk after
chunk of him disappeared. Faster and faster,
more and more chunks of him just…vanished…

"Captain! Hey, Captain!"

"JOHN!"

Lisa's yell broke through the vision. A
flash of light reflected from the silver
cross around her neck. She was inches away,
looking straight into my eyes.

The concern I saw there vanished in an
instant. Kawalski stood next to her, looking
puzzled.

"He's okay, Sergeant. Would you be a dear
and get me two more specimen bags from my car
please?"

"Sure, Doc. You, you sure he's all right?"

"I'm sure."

I didn't hear Kawalski's footsteps echo

down the alley. I was looking into those gorgeous eyes. Just like I'd done a thousand times before…

The stench from the dumpster and the blood wouldn't let me sink into that memory.

Damn.

"You saw it, didn't you?"

"Yes."

"Well?"

"There was nothing there."

"John," she cupped my face in her hands, "what do you mean?"

I was glad she'd seen me like this before. She knew how to guide me back.

Slowly.

Gently.

Quietly.

Safely.

She also knew when I was all the way back. Her arms went to her hips, and anger grew in those beautiful eyes until I had to look away.

Just like before.

Damn.

"He chased her to there," I pointed to her body. "He kissed her neck for a long time. Then he stabbed her. He was angry, hateful. Evil. He killed her and then he stood there, panting. He," I stopped long enough to swallow Harlem, "he was licking her blood from the knife when something hit him. A chunk of him was gone. Like you said, as if it was bitten off of him. But nothing was there. Then he was hit, bitten, whatever it was. Again and again, faster and faster, driving him over to there." I pointed to the murderer's body.

"John, something had to…"

"There was just a, well, a blur, a ripple

in the air, like hot air rising off of the asphalt. Nothing else, Lisa."

Saying her name brought a lump up. Two lumps.

"Lisa. I…"

"Don't."

Cold.

Ice.

Damn.

She had turned back to the woman's body already. Kawalski's steps echoed closer.

Yeah, this was going to be a long day.

Back at the precinct, waiting for my partner, I'd sat at my desk. I shoved the thirty-five alerts about terrorists targeting trains and busses into the round file. I needed room to begin the process of getting the victim's ID, her address, whatever we had on her. I was laying the foundation for the day while I waited for my partner to come in. When she got here, we'd plan the legwork and then begin the slog.

My eyes were still complaining about the lack of sleep. I rubbed them for a few seconds.

The gentle touch of her lips on mine opened my eyes. Her scent made me smile.

Comfortable.

Familiar.

Electric.

I gazed deeply into those eyes. A shiver passed through me at the sight of the love there.

"Wake up Martin." Deputy Inspector Alice MacDonald slammed the coffee down hard on my desk. How she didn't crumple the Styrofoam cup, I don't know.

"Mac, you sure can ruin a good dream."

"Can it. I need to know what you think

happened out there." She'd heard me. "In my office. Now."

Damn.

"Yes, Inspector." I hate being woken up by angry women.

It seems to happen to me a lot though.

I checked the clock as I fell into the cheap seats in MacDonald's office. Hell, they were all cheap seats in her office. Except hers. Hmm. Three thirty A-friggin'-M. Already.

"Well?"

"The guy grabbed, kissed, and stabbed the girl. Something…" I couldn't think of a better word, "ate most of the guy." I flinched, waiting to get hit by the Mac truck.

"Is that a guess, or did you…"

She didn't have to finish the question. She knew. Lisa knew. I think half of the NYPD knew. They just never talked about it. I took a deep breath.

"Yeah. I saw it."

MacDonald deflated into her overstuffed chair. Hey, rank has its privileges.

"Tell me."

So I told her. Everything. Including the 'nothing' that…

"Nothing? Really, John?"

"That's it, Mac. It's what I saw. I can't explain it."

"The guy's father is the Mayor's nephew, a ward supervisor. He wants answers. The Mayor wants answers. What do I tell them? That a 'ripple of air' ate him?"

"Tell them he killed the woman, we've got his prints on the murder weapon. Tell them we're looking for what killed him."

"WHAT killed him?" She stood up. I hate it

6

when women stand to yell at me. That seems to happen to me a lot lately, too.

"Mac, that's what I saw. I can't change it." The lack of both sleep and caffeine had given me a headache.

She sat down. A good sign. I took a gulp of coffee. She squinted at me.

Not a good sign.

"What do you THINK it was?"

Damn!

"Something invisib…"

"WHAT!" She stood up again.

"Mac, you asked me what I…"

"I need something I can use Martin! Damn it!"

I took a deep breath.

"Mac, I don't know. Me seeing crimes doesn't make sense, but you, and others, seem to accept it. This isn't any different. I can't control it, or change the view, or ask questions." I hate clichés, but all I could think of to say was, "It is what it is."

Mac still squinted at me. I almost turned around to see if there was a bright light behind me.

She took in a big breath.

"What's your best guess?"

Now, that surprised me. So I took a deep breath.

"Something-invisible-ate-him."

Mac looked at me. Stared, really. For about twenty seconds. It felt like an hour.

"Can you give me something I can use?"

"Say we're still searching for the killer. It's honest."

"Hmm. Okay. John."

Oh, no. First name.

Damn.

"Not a word. To anyone. No going public if you don't like the direction of the investigation. Understood?"

"Uh, yeah, sure, Inspector. You've got it." I took a big gulp of coffee.

"All right. Get back to work."

I stood to head back to my desk. Hey, I've worked here long enough to know that 'go get busy someplace else' tone.

I looked at my desk from the doorway of Mac's office. Patty was there, sitting on the corner of my desk. Legs crossed. Dark blue jacket, medium blue shirt, dark blue hose under a dark blue skirt cut just above the knee. All under brilliant golden hair.

Now, there's nothing wrong with Patty. And that's the problem. Her figure is perfect. Her face is perfect. Her hair, her eyes, perfect. Her IQ is over one-fifty. She's confident, but not aggressive. More confident than any new detective I've ever seen. Bold, not squeamish, but sensible, and always under control.

Perfect.

She's been my partner for two years, three months, and four days. I'll always remember. I've been divorced for two years, two months, and four days.

"Everything all right, partner?"

Did I mention her voice?

Perfect.

"Yeah, Patty. Mac just wanted the lowdown on the alley mess. We should start the legwork. You ready?"

"Sure. You drive."

"Sure. I'll fill you in as we go."

"I brought you some coffee. Figured you'd need it." She stretched her five foot ten inch frame off of the desk, arms up high. Back arched.

8

Damn!

She's the only NYPD detective who wears uniform skirts. She looked like she had heels on, but she didn't. She never even wore makeup, but she still stopped traffic when she crossed the street.

"Um, thanks, Patty." I grabbed my coat. Still wet. I held it in front of me. It had turned into one of those days. You know, when the universe fights you on every step you take.

Patty turned towards the elevator and started walking.

Damn.

There's a reason old time etiquette had the women walking *behind* the men. The reason's called Patricia Margaret Theresa O'Rourke. I managed a glance around. All twenty-six eyes in the office followed that gentle sway as it drifted out the door. Eighteen of them were male. I didn't dare look back to check Mac's office. Some things I never want to know.

I grabbed the coffee and followed her.

I always drove. Patty always suggested it. It was just the way it happened.

Every time, on every case.

I told her a little about the bodies as I drove. Mostly I drank the coffee.

And thought how I'd feel better if it was Scotch.

We parked outside the alley. Patty waited for me by my old Crown Vic's front fender. I walked down the alley and she followed, about a half step behind me. We'd never talked about it, but it's the way we always approached a crime scene.

"She was here. He was there."

Patty looked around. I looked around. Chalk lines over bloodstains. Pretty

9

standard.

"Did you…"

"Yeah."

Patty snapped her head around. She was always concerned when I saw a crime. Like I was going to be hurt by it. Or go crazy over it.

"You should have told me in the car. Are you…okay?"

"I don't know." My answer surprised me. "Lisa was here." I was staring at my shoes. A shadow made me look up.

Patty was inches away. I could smell her. Not perfume, she never wore any. Just…her. Like fresh rain.

Perfect.

Damn!

"Tell me."

So I went over it.

Again.

I saw crimes, Patty saw people. Not reading their minds, exactly. More like a sense of what they were feeling. We never talked about it directly. I just sort of picked up on it.

"John, you're worried because you didn't see what killed him, aren't you?"

"Yeah, I guess…"

Something buzzed past my ear. I reached up and swatted the air.

Patty had moved to the left, searching the alley in the direction the buzzing went. Another something flew between us. It was just a blur, a ripple in the air. Patty tried to follow it with her eyes. So did I.

Nothing.

"John, did you…"

"Sort of. I lost it."

I looked at Patty. She was calm and cool

as always. And she was white as a ghost.

"Hey, you okay?"

She looked at me and shook her head.

"We need to hurry. This is not right. Something's not…good."

I was frozen. Apart from her perfect looks, Patty was tough. I've seen her stare down hit men, mob bosses, and Secret Service agents.

She'd even set that masher of a President in his place.

Seeing her spooked scared me.

She walked the perimeter of the alley, looking up and down the walls. She went back to the dumpster and peered behind it for about twenty seconds. She motioned me over and we met over the woman's chalk outline.

"Don't worry about what killed the man. Why did he kill the woman?"

"I didn't see that."

"No, I mean we need to know why he did it. We still have to prove he did it."

"Yeah, we'd better get moving on that before Mac pops a vein."

We walked out of the alley, following the direction the woman ran from.

I checked the addresses we walked past with the one I'd found for the woman, Agnes Valparaiso. I had it memorized, but it gave me a chance to check on Patty. She seemed her usual self now.

Something else caught my eye. Blood. Even with the drizzling rain, there were places it lingered. Sidewalk cracks, red puddles. The stoop to the victim's building was under an awning. The rain hadn't washed the blood away there.

And there was a lot of it.

Did I mention I hated blood?

We followed the trail back to the woman's apartment. Kawalski had the building's super there, just inside the open door. I walked in, Patty right behind me. I heard her gasp at the same time the scene registered in my brain.

I fought hard to keep last night's pizza and Scotch down.

I won't say that there was blood everywhere. It wouldn't be far off if I did, though. There was enough to keep the floor sticky and slippery.

"Captain, there's two more bodies. One in the kitchen, another in the bedroom." Kawalski's a big, tough looking guy, but he sounded rattled.

I don't blame him.

Patty spoke first.

"Who's the tee-shirt, Kawalski?"

"Terry Moran, Officer. I'm the super in this building."

Aside from the metallic scent of blood, Mr. Moran carried the strongest odor in the room.

He smelled like pigeons.

"Pleased to meet you. Kawalski, take him outside and get his statement. Find out if he heard anything last night."

"Yes, Ma'am."

"I'll be right here."

I watched Patty close the door behind them. She slid the deadbolt closed.

My feet slipped a few times as I went to the bedroom door. Standing with my back to the jam, I scanned the bedroom, the living room, and the kitchen areas. Another deep breath, then I closed my eyes as I let it out.

The two women moved over the guy on the

bed. They seemed to be in a contest to see who could remove more of his clothing. Agnes held up his wallet so the other woman could see it, but the guy couldn't. The other woman laughed and rolled on top of the guy.

Agnes got up and went to the fire escape. She opened the window, and the guy from the alley came in. Agnes offered him the wallet, but he slapped it out of her hand. He went to the bed and threw the other woman against the far wall like yesterday's spaghetti. With one hand. The guy on the bed started to get up, but Mr. Alley backhanded him unconscious.

Then he bent down and bit the guy's neck.

Agnes screamed and ran into the kitchen. Mr. Alley went over to the first woman, still slumped against the wall, and picked her up with one hand. He carried her into the living room, biting her neck as he moved.

Agnes slammed a large knife into the guy. He screamed and flung the first woman against the wall again, blood spraying everywhere from her neck. In the same motion he grabbed Agnes' arm, pulling her to him. He bit her neck as she stabbed him again. He released her and screamed, and she ran out of the apartment.

Mr. Alley followed.

"John, I need you. John!"

"What…"

The room was spinning around me. Fast. Something huge and pale moved towards me. Big, pale, and ugly. With teeth. Patty's voice was fading away. I started to panic.

I was caught in between…

"John! Snap out of it!"

The slap stung my cheek.

I blinked my eyes. Twice. The room was way too bright. Then the flashlight moved off of my face, and I could see those eyes.

Damn.

Lisa looked at me, the worried look fading as she realized I was back. I watched those eyes become very angry as she turned away from me.

"Don't you ever let him do that unless I'm here. And bolting that door. Are you just stupid, or are you trying to…"

Patty stared wide-eyed as Lisa cut short her tirade and took a step toward her.

"I, I just, I…" Patty stumbled on her words.

That never happened.

"You will never replace me in any way. Is that clear!" Lisa hissed.

Patty nodded her head.

Lisa turned back to me.

Damn.

2

We didn't have a lot of real evidence. But when you know the story behind it, you know what's important and what to ignore. We had enough.

We had the DNA on the knife from the guy. We had Agnes' body. And the two in the apartment. The guy's DNA was all over them, especially the saliva in the bite marks.

But Lisa said the saliva and the DNA were…unusual. Something in the saliva stopped blood from clotting. And the guy's DNA matched, but there was something…extra in it.

Anything unusual or extra about evidence is a problem.

So there we were, Lisa, Patty, and me. In Mac's office. Me in no-man's-land between Patty and Lisa. In Mac's tiny little lunchbox of an office.

"How did this happen?" Mac wanted an explanation. Yeah, like I changed the guy's DNA.

"Well, Mac, the DNA in the sperm and the DNA…"

"Can it! How does someone get anticoagulant saliva?"

"Maybe that's what the extra DNA is for."

"Yeah, where did that come from? Not the guy's parents. Did he do time at Three Mile Island or Chernobyl or something? Was he abducted by aliens? A government experiment?"

"Inspector, these are valid questions, but we are not the ones to ask…"

Patty's perfect reputation just cracked.

"YOU are PRE – CISE - LY the people to ask these questions! YOU should ALL be asking them until you can bring me some DAMN answers! Now get moving!"

Hmm. Mac usually went on for an hour on something like this.

Maybe that was the perfect response after all.

Now to see if I can get Lisa and Patty out of the office without World War Three breaking out.

To my surprise the two stood, turned and walked out without a word or even a glance at each other.

In my experience there's no such thing as a 'good omen'.

There are only fate's cruel set-ups.

The two made it three steps past Mac's door. Lisa stopped and turned to face Patty. I'd seen that expression before.

I looked for a foxhole to dive into.

She looked right past me.

At Patty.

Lisa's mouth opened, but the words came from behind me.

"Don't you have some research to do, DOCTOR Martin?"

Yeah, Mac had her gloves off, and she was waving a full set of well polished brass knuckles under Lisa's nose.

Lisa closed her mouth and stared at Mac.

"Well, Doctor?"

Lisa turned and walked out of the office.

Damn!

I looked from Patty to Mac. Patty the boxer, waiting for the ten count on her opponent. Mac looked like…

Mac.

"Get me some answers, John." She winked.

I drove us to the Harlem DNA lab. Patty rode shotgun. She gave no indication of being upset, concerned, amused, or even interested in what Lisa would have said to her.

16

Me? I was worried. Worried that Lisa's 'research' would bring her here too. I scanned the parking lot as I drove in.

It was a big parking lot.

We signed in at the desk. I looked at the registry.

No Dr. Martins.

The office of Dr. Clemens Montrose was on the seventh floor. The good doctor greeted us like we were week-old sushi.

"Detective. How can you have 'extra' DNA? The media really has gone too far with this populist reporting of junk scien…"

I tossed the test results on the desk in front of him.

"Dr. Montrose, the tests were done here. I was hoping *you* could explain to *us* what the results mean."

"Ahh! This is the one! Yes, yes! I verified these results myself. Quite unusual. Quite."

"But, what do the results mean?"

Every piece of metal and plastic in the room softened and melted.

Patty could do that with her voice.

The doctor swallowed hard as he stared at Patty, who took the opportunity to cross her legs. Very slowly.

"Well, Miss…"

"Detective O'Rourke." Patty's eyes batted as if they spoke the words.

"Ahem. Yes. Eh, Miss, eh…"

Patty nodded once, then used her tongue to wipe the slight smile flickering across her glistening lips.

"Well, Miss O'Rourke, this pattern suggests a recent mutation of the subject's DNA. There were changes to the areas responsible for muscle development and the

17

digestive process, as well as dentations."
The doctor licked his lips and sat back, very
pleased with himself.

Patty leaned forward.

When did she unbutton the top of her
blouse?

"And, doc-torrrrr," Catwoman, eat your
heart out! "How could this happen? What would
have caused it?" Three bats of the eyelashes.

I'd never seen Patty turn it up *this* high.

Except that time with the President…

This guy was toast. Hell, right now I was
toast.

"AH-HEM!"

Damn!

Now I *was* toast.

"Ah, Lisa, er, um, Dr. Martin! Come in!
Please, eh, Lisa, dear, please come in! We
were just uh, er, discussing the item you
called me about!" Montrose stood up behind
his desk, but not all the way.

Interesting!

"I heard, Clem. The *detective* asked a good
question. How did this happen?"

Okay, it could be worse.

"Oh, eh, Lisa, well, ahem… You see, a
genetic modification agent would have to be
introduced system wide within a short period
of time. The changes would have been very
painful. But once done, irreversible!"

I looked from Dr. Montrose, to Lisa, to
Patty. Hmm.

Lisa was mad.

But not at me.

Or Patty.

Montrose was…

The cat with the canary feather stuck in
his teeth.

18

I almost felt sorry for the guy.

Well, I'll be damned. Lisa had a little playmate!

I noticed Patty grinning. Some ancient instinct kicked in, and I decided the best way to protect Lisa was to make a graceful exit.

"Thank you, Dr. Montrose. That was very helpful." I turned and tipped my hat at Lisa, "Dr. Martin." I couldn't help but leave that not-so-subtle reminder in the room. Montrose's eyes got real big.

I nodded in Patty's direction.

"Goodbye, Doctor *baby!*" Patty batted her lashes before she turned and swayed her… hips out of the room.

Perfect!

I had just put the old Crown Vic into Drive when the radio cracked.

"Captain Martin, proceed to 6th Avenue and Broadway. Interview witnesses there."

Damn.

The upscale neighborhood looked downscale with six police cruisers flashing away. A dozen people stood near one car.

Kowalski pushed through the crowd to the Crown Vic.

"Captain Martin, these people saw the mugging. You need to hear their story, Cap."

Kowalski was way too excited for a mugging.

"Why are we being diverted to a mugging from a murder investigation?"

"Just listen, Cap. I've had the guys keep 'em separated, just like you taught me. Here, the victim..."

"Angela Halliburton. Detective...?"

"Captain Martin, Ma'am. My partner, Patricia O'Rourke. Tell us what happened."

19

The high society type looked flustered.
Scared.

"The man grabbed my purse, and pulled a knife on me. He asked for my necklace, my rings..."

Diamonds.

A lot of diamonds.

"Then he just..."

She began sobbing.

"It's all right, Mrs. Halliburton. Just tell me what happened." Patty wrapped her arm around the lady.

"It was as if something... ate him. A bite at a time. He screamed, and then..."

"All the others tell the same story, Cap. The body's over this way."

I followed Kowalski to the side of a subway kiosk.

Damn.

Well, at least the guy's feet were intact.

"Get their statements, Kowalski. Good work."

I sat in the car for three minutes.

"Are you all right, John?"

Yeah, this was a long day all right.

"Time for lunch."

We stopped at Allessandros' and I bought Patty lunch. The show at the lab had been worth $12.75. The clock behind the counter said it was 10:10 AM. The 24-hour news channel on the TV was showing some Columbia scientist with an empty cage.

Make that an almost empty cage.

The air inside the cage… rippled.

I spilled my coffee.

"Gladys, turn up the TV!" Patty looked at me like I'd grown a third head. I'd sprayed bits of chewed gyro all over the counter.

"Calm down, John. You'll choke to death one of these days." Gladys hit the remote and wiped up my mess. She set a fresh coffee in front of me.

She knew I'd double her tip.

"…and, Dr. Wattson, these creatures are a totally new species?"

"Yes, but more than that." The camera zoomed in on the foot long cage. "They are totally unlike any other life on Earth! They don't fit into any zoological classification. Not only are they nearly transparent, but their metabolism is totally different. And their DNA…."

Something shimmered in the cage. It looked about six inches long, and it…

Rippled.

Damn!

"Here is a close-up, slow motion capture of the creature." A six inch long transparent tube with an inch wide skirt that rippled slowly along the length of it filled the screen. It reminded me of a squid.

"These creatures eat a *lot* of food," Dr. Wattson piled a ton of emphasis on 'lot,' "to keep their metabolic levels so high."

As if to emphasize the point, the thing turned toward the camera and opened its mouth. Piranha-like teeth flashed before snapping shut with a loud 'crack'.

Damn!

"Grab your lunch, Patty. We'll eat in the car."

I glanced at Patty as I stood up. Her mouth was gaping and her eyes were wider than a 52 Packard's hubcaps.

"PATTY!"

"Yeah, right. You drive, okay boss?" She kept her eyes on the TV until we were outside of the restaurant.

21

I used the siren all the way. It still took us an hour and a half to get there. Patty stared straight ahead the whole time.

It took us another half hour to find where Dr. Wattson's office was. We walked up to the mousy receptionist sitting behind the almost-wood desk.

"May I help you?"

"Ghostbusters, right?" I could feel Patty's eyelashes flutter. Three times, "You were in the Ghostbusters movies!"

The mousy receptionist looked up at Patty. Patty flashed her smile, and the receptionist blushed.

"We're looking for Dr. Wattson."

"Third door on the right, down the hallway to your left." She batted her eyes at Patty.

"Thank you. Thank you very much!"

I opened the door to the professor's office and held it for Patty.

Nothing like leading with your best punch.

"No more interviews! I've done six today. NO MO…"

"Not an interview for the press, Dr." I flashed my badge in his direction for a full quarter second. He wasn't looking.

"Eh, wha… who… police?"

It sunk in eventually.

Patty had that effect on people.

"We saw you on TV. We need some information on the creatures you've discovered." I tried to make it sound routine.

I failed.

He didn't notice.

"Eh… Creatures…" Wattson couldn't get past staring at Patty. I began to wonder if his eyes would ever get up to her face.

"Professor, may we see the little ol'

thing?"

Patty batted her eyes again.

These science types seem to go for that.

"Uh, yeah, sure. It's over here. It's dead now. Don't know why." Wattson motioned to his right. On a medical drainage pad laid the creature, a translucent milky white now.

"What is it, Doc?" It was the best I could come up with.

"It's an animal. Mostly muscle. It eats other animals, and some high energy plant matter. Other than that…"

"Does it have a name?" I shot a glance at Patty. She'd been unusually quiet since she spotted the creature. She looked too serious.

"All I could come up with is Rods."

"What? Rods? You mean like those optical illusions that show up in outdoor pictures from time to time? I thought those were all just insects blurred by the camera."

"Most. Not all. I've found a place near New Rochelle. I've filmed them. A lot of them."

"What do you mean, a lot of them?"

"There are dozens, hundreds flying around at twilight. Here, let me bring the video up," Wattson began fussing on his computer. "The air is full of them. There seems to be several different shapes. I don't know if they are different species or genders or…"

"There are six different types." We both snapped our eyes to Patty.

"Yes, yes! Rods, ribbons, spirals, darts, barrels, and, disks. How did you know?" Wattson was gazing at Patty with enthusiasm now.

"I, it was a lucky guess." Patty seemed flustered as she stared at the video.

I didn't like that.

Not one bit.

I looked at the dead rod on the lab bench. The mouth was open. I reached out to touch those teeth…

"DON'T!" Wattson yelled as he grabbed my wrist. "Those teeth have a molecular edge."

"Molecular edge? What's that?"

"The cutting edge is one molecule thick. And even that molecule has an edge on it. And the molecule vibrates. One touch could slice your finger off." He held up his left hand and wiggled a bandaged thumb at me. "I was lucky."

"Say, Doc, did you happen to film these things feeding at all?"

"Yeah. It's kind of…" he looked at Patty, worried, "..disturbing."

"Show me." I had to see it. I had to know if these were what ate the perp.

I looked at Patty. She nodded. Like she already knew.

"By the way, what's all this about, anyway? These aren't an endangered species, or some government bio-weapon project that got loose, are they?"

"No, Doc. We're investigating a murder."

"Murder!"

Everyone always repeated the word, like they'd never heard it before.

Every time.

"The murderer ended up looking like…" The video took my voice. A goat carcass was hung from a tree. In less than twenty seconds there was nothing left but a skeleton.

"…just like that! Damn!"

"Where was this murder?"

"Two. Harlem. The better part. And Midtown."

"I didn't think they'd range that far.

24

There must be another colony. I've got to find them." Wattson began stuffing cameras and some other equipment into a duffle bag. "You've got to take me there."

"Now, hold on Professor. That's a crime scen…"

"You can ride in the back. I'll drive." Patty grabbed his arm and headed back to the car.

Damn!

By the time the shock of Patty saying she'd drive wore off they were out of sight. I had to run to catch them.

Did I mention that I hate running?

"Hey. Patty!" She turned around as I panted behind her.

"Do you even have a driver's license?"

"I don't need one. I'm a cop. Remember?"

I squinted at her. Ice-cold was a familiar look for the women in my life.

"Yeah, well. I'll drive." I pushed past her and opened the driver's door. "Let's go then." I nodded towards the other side of the car.

She was already there.

Patty opened the door and Wattson piled into the back seat. A second later Patty was sitting next to me.

"Well, John, move it!"

I stared at her for a moment, then started the car.

Yeah. This was gunna be a long day.

Somewhere along the way Patty stuck the flasher on the roof of the car. I took the hint.

New York City traffic isn't anywhere near as bad as people make it out to be.

Unless you want to get some place.

A mile from the alley, traffic turned into

a brick wall.

I could feel Patty fidgeting in her seat. But just for a moment.

"Hey! Patty, what…"

She was already outside and opening the back door for Wattson. He grabbed his equipment and they disappeared.

Damn.

Twenty minutes later, I parked near the entrance to the alley. Patty stood watching Wattson as he pointed some electronic gadget at various items in the alley. Patty kept an eye on that hole behind the dumpster in a way that the professor wouldn't notice.

"Well, did you find the sweet little nothings?" I hit my partner with the veteran-scolding-the-rookie stare.

"No. Yes. No." Wattson never looked away from his gizmo. Patty gave me the apology look.

"There are no Rods in this alley." The professor hit a switch on the gadget and the little lights went dark. He looked around the alley twice before tilting his head and squinting at me. "Are you sure you saw them here?"

"Twice. Doc, do me a favor. Point your gizmo behind the dumpster."

"Sure." He powered the thing up and walked to the dumpster, moving the tip of his contraption as if he was spraying something. After twenty seconds he turned his machine off.

"Nope. They're not here."

"John, are you sure?"

"Yes. And you saw them too, remember?" I sounded grumpier than I meant to.

"Can you look again, to be sure?" Patty's voice was almost a whisper. She glanced around as if looking for…

Her eyes told me she didn't like asking me to do this. She never liked asking me to do this. And after the debacle in the apartment earlier, with Lisa's warning…

I glanced at Wattson. He sent a confused look in Patty's direction.

"Yeah. Sure. Why not." All I needed was some lab jockey studying my visions. I took in a deep breath and sighed.

Maybe that was what I needed.

I walked over to the brick wall again. I pressed my back into the damp bricks, spread my arms, and scanned the alley.

I heard Patty's voice saying something, to the professor I think. I saw him point that gizmo at me.

I took a deep breath and closed my eyes…

She was sobbing as she ran down the street. Panicked, terrified. Blood was running from down her neck, thinned by the rain. She nearly fell when she turned into the alley. He was close behind her, knife held high. He caught up with her at the dumpster. He grabbed her, pulled her close. She went limp as he kissed her neck. Five, ten, twenty seconds he held the kiss before he pulled back. Twice the knife came down into her neck before she turned. He kept stabbing, twice more on her arm, twice on her face, then twice on her chest. I could feel the evil pouring out of him wash over me as I watched the blood pour out of her.

He stood panting over her, hands on knees. His mouth was covered with her blood. He licked the knife and his lips clean. He stood up tall and smiled. Then he jerked back, as if he'd been hit. Blood fell from a hole in his forehead. He jerked back again, a second wound bleeding on his neck. He screamed as a third, then a fourth wound drove him back. Another strike, then another, then he was

against the brick wall, sliding down, as
chunk after chunk of him disappeared. Faster
and faster, more and more chunks of him just…
vanished…

A loud crack and the vision vanished.

I was always thankful when I came out of a
vision.

They were always gruesome.

I wish I had stayed in this time.

My partner was sitting in a puddle,
rubbing her cheek.

Lisa glared over Patty, her face almost as
enraged as that guy with the knife.

Patty looked up, then stood. She looked
Lisa straight in the eyes.

"This one time. No more." Then she leaned
close and said something I could not hear.

Lisa tilted her head and squinted at
Patty. She held the pose for an eternity that
lasted probably ten seconds.

"Sorry. I didn't know."

Damn!

"That was AMAZING! How did you do that?"

The three of us turned to stare at
Wattson.

"There were at least two hundred here!
They came down this way, from some place up
there," He pointed up, his finger moving in
circles, "and swooped down on the…"

Sometimes it takes a few minutes for
things to register with people.

The professor's eyes grew wide. He was
looking right at the blood stained pavement
with the chalk outline. He dropped his gizmo
and ran over to the dumpster.

He bent over and blew lunch.

Lisa glanced at me, and then went over to
Wattson.

That's when Patty's cell phone rang.

3

"I said come on!" She grabbed my hand and began a fast walk to the car. "I'm driving. Professor, you too!"

A long day for sure.

I fastened my seatbelt.

Hey, I'd never ridden shotgun to Patty before.

"Where are we going?"

"Upstate. It's about a three-hour drive. Get some sleep."

I knew that 'no room for negotiation' tone. I'd never heard it from Patty before though. She seemed, well, different since this morning in the alley.

So I went to sleep.

I used to like sleep. No screaming ex-wives. No alimony. No cranky bosses. No murders flashing before my eyes.

Just Lisa.

The good Lisa.

The two kids ran across the meadow. A boy and a girl. They looked like brother and sister. About ten and eight I'd say. Flowers blooming, sun shining. Warm. Birds singing. Sweet smelling air.

Nice.

Like a good dream.

Except for the cougar stalking them.

The big cat crouched at the edge of the meadow, haunches shivering. It was going to…

"NO!"

The shoulder harness cut into my neck.

"WHAT?" Patty screamed as she hit the brakes hard.

"Ow!" Wattson's head hit the plexiglass wall behind my seat.

"Kids. Meadow. Cougar, big cat, mountain lion, stalking…" My heart was pounding and I couldn't catch my breath.

"It was a dream, John."

She didn't sound convinced.

"I don't think so."

I heard her gulp. I looked at her.

She was nervous.

A horn blared as a car flashed past us.

"Patty…"

"Close your eyes. It could still be there."

"I don't want to."

"Do it. I need to know…"

That tone again.

Damn.

Something blurred across the meadow, behind the kids. Like a ripple in the air. More ripples followed.

A lot more.

The big cat's hindquarters began quivering…

The loose group of ripples curved up and behind the kids. Then they began diving.

When the ripples went back up, the cat was gone.

I followed the ripples now. They moved towards the kids.

The horn from another passing car saved me. I looked at Patty.

"Please, no." I was scared.

Sweating.

Shaking.

"Do it."

Damn.

I swallowed a really big lump of nothing and closed my eyes.

The ripples went over the kids. I swear my

heart stopped. *The ripples kept going. After a few hundred yards they went into a cave.*

I felt my heart beat.

Thank you Lord.

My throat tightened when the kids came to the cave entrance. They stopped just outside the opening. The girl held up a cell phone and the boy reached into his pocket. He pulled out a chocolate bar, unwrapped it and held up.

The two kids giggled as the air rippled and the chocolate disappeared. Completely. Not even a smudge was left on the kid's untouched hand.

The ripples went back into the cave. The two kids started skipping away, giggling as they went.

Then it went dark.

I opened my eyes. I was shaking. I didn't want to know, but I asked anyway.

"We're going to that cave, aren't we?"

Patty nodded her head once.

The day just got a lot longer.

That's when Patty's cell phone rang.

She pulled it off of her belt and handed it to me.

I looked at the screen.

It was Mac's office.

"Martin here."

The silence lasted ten seconds.

"Where is O'Rourke? Is she all right?"

"Mac! Nice to hear from you, too. Patty's driving."

The silence lasted twelve seconds this time. Not good.

"Why is she driving? She never drives. You always drive. Where are you going? Are you all right? Is she all right?"

"She asked to drive. Upstate following a lead. Yes, I'm fine, thanks. Yes, she is fine too."

"Damn it, John, stop playing games. I've got something for you two. Turn around."

Mac was loud enough for Patty to hear. She glanced my way, squinting.

Mac was waiting for some kind of response.

I was calculating if I could afford to retire.

Today.

Running the numbers didn't take long.

I didn't like the answer.

"Get your butts to Bellevue Ave North in Yonkers. The school there has been…" Mac at a loss for words. I heard her swallow.

Hard.

Not good.

"… attacked."

My head almost hit the dashboard when Patty stomped on the brakes.

"Ow!" Thud. Wattson must have a good sized knot by now.

"Check it out and call me." Mac hung up.

"Damn it, Patty. You're never driving again."

"NO! It's too soon! I'm not ready!"

Patty was staring straight up. A tear ran down her cheek.

I glanced at Wattson. He sat like a statue. A pale statue with a big blue lump on his forehead.

I turned to my partner.

"Hey, you okay?"

She looked at me. Her eyes were worried. Really worried.

"Let's go. Be ready for…"

She never finished.

She just drove.

Fast.

Damn fast.

The locals brought us around behind the school. I looked up at the scene and almost lost it again.

I turned away to regroup.

After a few minutes, I thought I had control back.

I looked out over the scene and almost lost lunch again.

Damn.

At least it wasn't raining.

When the spasm stopped, I brushed the snow off of my shoulders.

"It was gym class. Thirty kids. Sixth graders. And their teacher, Mr. Alverez…"

Kids.

I felt dizzy. I looked for a place to sit down.

Or a cave to crawl into.

All I saw was a big, steaming red-black stain on the grass. And about a dozen arms and legs.

Small arms and legs.

Damn.

I took a deep breath.

I took another deep breath.

Then another.

A lot of deep breaths.

I glanced at Patty.

Yeah.

Deep breaths.

Patty turned to the local cops. Her jaw was tight. Her knuckles were white. Something fierce burned behind those perfect eyes.

"Okay. We need to go over the crime scene. I need you to keep everyone out by the street in front of the school. Out of our way."

When they had left us alone, she nodded to Wattson and then turned to me.

"Patty. They're kids. I can't…"

"John…"

"Please don't ask…"

"I have to know."

Damn.

I walked to the nearest wall of the school. I took a deep breath. I looked over the field as I let the breath out.

Then I closed my eyes.

Thirty of them, eleven and twelve year old kids. Twenty two of them lined up for a flag football play, the rest on the sidelines waiting their turn to get in the game. The gym teacher at the ready, hands on knees, whistle in his teeth.

Then the shadow fell across him…

The thing was big. Pinkish-grey belly, the rest a blotchy, almost black shade of red. About twenty feet long. Arms, legs, wings, forked tail. Claws. Hooves. Horns. Teeth. It took half of one team with the first bite. The upper half. The rest took about ten seconds. When it was over, it flew off, flying low, awkwardly weaving through the trees.

The screams kept echoing in my ears.

Over.

And over.

And over again…

I don't know how long I was out.

Lisa was there when I came back.

Patty must have called her.

"John."

Fingers brushing my hair.

Tenderness in her tone and her touch.

34

It had to be a dream.

"John. Wake up."

I opened my eyes.

I'd do anything to bathe in that tenderness for as long as it lasted. After a dozen seconds or so, I watched the tenderness fade like a shadow when you turn on the lights.

No dream.

Damn.

Lisa turned to Patty. She's usually cold to me, but the look she shot Patty would start an ice age.

"You should have never made him do that. Not with kids."

"Wh-what? Why..."

"His little brother. John was twelve, James was ten. They were at the airport, waiting for John's father to land. They were going to surprise him. James broke away from John's hand and ran out onto the runway. Into the propeller."

"It's okay."

Both of them looked at me.

"Tell me what you saw." Patty's voice cracked a little.

"It was a demon. Or a gargoyle. Both fit."

Patty looked at me as if I'd just told her that her dog, her parents, and her kids were dead.

Lisa looked at me like…

Damn.

"Lisa, maybe you should help the Professor. I'll be okay."

Wattson was finishing his dry heaves by the corner of the school.

Lisa ignored me.

She'd gotten pretty good at that.

Patty sat down on the grass. Lisa looked at her, then me. The concern was back in her eyes.

"What's going on here? What do you two know?"

Patty had her face in her hands, rocking and mumbling "too soon" and "Lord, give me strength" over and over again. She wasn't the rock I'd had for a partner the past two years. She was shaken up pretty bad.

And she hadn't had to watch what happened.

That sort of ticked me off.

I sat up and slid over next to her. I could feel Lisa's ice-dagger glances but I let it go as I snapped my fingers in front of my partner's face.

"Patty! Damn it, Patty."

She was shaking.

I clapped my hands an inch in front of her nose.

"PATTY!"

She looked up at me, surprised.

"You know something." I needed to be a NYPD captain again. I hadn't used the 'boss tone' in a long time. "There's something about this place. And what happened in the alley. They're connected. Tell me."

"This, thing. That did this. It's… There will be…too soon! I'm not ready!"

She went back into her shell.

Lisa bent over, her silver cross catching the sunlight. She whispered in Patty's ear. Soft and tender. She pulled Patty up and helped her to the car.

Dragged her almost.

I saw Wattson staggering behind them.

I took a walk around the field, looking for something.

Footprints?

Scales?

Excalibur?

A magic amulet…

Anything to tell me I wasn't going nuts.

I tried not to look at the arms and legs.

I still don't know how Lisa does it.

Except that they weren't her brother's arms and legs…

Damn.

Two more M.E. vans were out front. Lisa and three others went to do their thing with the, um, parts out back.

News trucks pulled up in front of the school, so I left. Reporters have a bad habit of repeating everything I say. In the absolute worst context possible.

It was a quiet ride back to the station. Too quiet. Wattson slept. Patty just rocked in her seat.

There was a decent parking spot in the garage, so I wouldn't have to drag my partner too far. I got out and walked around the car. As I opened her door the thought hit me; I'd never touched Patty. Almost two and a half years, not a handshake, a pat on the shoulder, a fist bump or a high five. Nothing.

Why couldn't I convince Lisa of that?

I reached in and took her hand.

The brightness almost knocked me down. It was like staring into a searchlight from a foot away. And the singing. But it wasn't quite singing. Patty turned and looked at me, smiled, put her feet on the pavement and stood up.

That's when I saw the wings.

The next thing I remember is sitting against the pillar a few feet from my Crown Vic. Patty was looking at me, her hand on my cheek.

The perfect Patty.

The gorgeous, smart, confident, in control Patty.

The one without the brilliant white wings.

"You all right, John?"

I managed to get to my feet.

"Maybe. Maybe I'm nuts."

Patty laughed.

"C'mon. You're not nuts."

Something felt different. Something…

James. It didn't rip my gut apart to think of James.

I looked at my partner.

My perfect partner.

Patty gave me a hand up and started walking to the elevator.

In front of me.

Damn!

I woke Wattson up. He grabbed his gizmos and we met Patty at the elevator.

The office was deserted, except for Mac. I glanced at the clock.

6 PM.

"Well?"

"You don't want to know."

Yeah, I've got a 'don't go there' tone too.

Only it's never worked with women.

Mac looked at me for twenty seconds.

"You saw it." Her whisper told me that she knew what happened out there.

I just nodded.

"John, Patty, I want you to see this, and tell me what you think." She had a remote in her hand. She clicked it.

The big screen TV on the wall woke up.

"Some call them 'Skyfish.' Some call them 'Rods.' Or 'Spirals.' They show up every now and then in photographs. Everyone swears they weren't there when the pictures were taken."

The narrator looked and sounded a little young to be playing the scientist type.

The screen showed image after image with translucent ripples in the air…

Ripples.

I glanced at Patty.

Then at Mac.

Both were looking at me.

"That's what killed the guy in the alley. That's what ate the cougar."

"Cougar?" Mac took a step back, looking a little pissed.

The guy on screen held something up.

"We managed to capture one. It died quickly, but we could still…"

The screen filled with video snow and static.

Then it went black.

"Wait, what was that?"

I had forgotten about Wattson.

"A Canadian documentary. It aired on CBC last night for twelve minutes before being cut off." Mac squinted at the professor.

"What do you mean, cut off? That doesn't make sense."

"Because he was about to mention the teeth." Wattson smiled and held out his hand to Mac, "Dr. Wattson, Miss…"

The professor had some charm after all.

"They aren't our problem."

Mac and I snapped our heads to face Patty.

"They're harmless to… good."

"They've killed five people, and thirty children." A six foot two inch dark suit

39

walked out of Mac's office. Kind of broad at the shoulders and narrow at the hips. Black fedora perfectly flat on his head. Every thing about him screamed FBI. Or NSA. Maybe DHS.

Or MIB.

Heh.

Sure.

Yeah, right.

I took a deep breath.

"Martin, O'Rourke," Mac glanced at Wattson, "Professor, there's someone you need to meet."

I had a feeling the day just got a whole lot longer.

I don't normally do the alpha male routine, but something about this guy made me straighten up a little as I squeezed the hand he offered.

Did I mention that I'm six feet five inches tall?

"Francis, Francis Herbert. S.I.S.S.I. Special Investigation Service for Scientific Inquiries."

"John Martin." I kept squeezing. Not hard, but he was going to let go first. "Nice to meet you, Francis Francis."

"John, play nice."

That perfect voice nearly melted every bone in my body. SISSI-boy gulped and pulled his hand back.

Did I mention that I have *the* perfect partner?

"Call me Freddy."

"What can I do for you, Freddy?"

"Patty, don't play *that* nice. Freddy, our own Doctor Wattson." I motioned past Patty to the professor. He was busy fussing with his gizmos.

"Here. Look at this." He flipped a switch on one of his gadgets and pressed a button on the TV.

It was the scene from the alley.

As I saw it.

Damn.

"How the hell did you…"

"JOHN MARTIN!" Patty was pissed.

At me.

Did I mention that happens a lot with women and me?

"Sorry. Forgive me, Father."

"Well, the frequency of the Rods' vibrations must have been tuned to… Actually, I don't know. I was scanning for Rods and this just… showed up on the screen. So I hit record."

Mac stared at the screen, and then shot a strange look at me.

"I got the scene at the school, too."

I could tell by the quiet way he said it that Wattson didn't want to say it.

The TV went black for a few seconds before the flag football game came on.

Damn.

I had to look away.

I knew it was over when I heard Freddy and Mac blowing lunch.

I looked at Wattson.

He looked at me.

He hadn't watched either.

Smart man.

I walked over to the coffee pot. Patty went to get the mop bucket for Mac and SISSI-boy. Wattson just stared at me.

"What?"

"How do you… Have you always…"

"I don't know and no. Anything else?"

"Yeah. Do you get used to…"

"No."

"Oh. Damn."

It was my turn to be confused.

"Why 'damn,' Doc?"

"I have a feeling there's going to be more. A lot more. I was hoping not to barf every time."

"What makes you think you'll be there if there is?" I started making some fresh coffee. If you could call what the Department sent us coffee.

"I'm your expert. You'll need me." He took a pack of gum out of his pocket and offered me a stick. I took it.

"Didn't you ever watch those '50s monster movies when you were a kid? The scientist always goes along."

"Why do you think there'll be more?"

The gum was Juicy Fruit.

I was beginning to like this egghead.

"First the Rods. Then the… thing at the school. They have to be connected. Something unusual is happening."

"I think you've been watching too many '50s monster flicks."

He looked at me like I had three heads.

"This from the guy who 'sees' crimes after they've happened?"

"Fair enough. Cream, sugar?"

"No cream. One sugar. Thanks." He took the mug I offered. I hoped Mac wouldn't mind. Or notice.

"So, what's your theory?"

Wattson looked at me like he was sizing me up for a bar fight. After a few seconds he nodded.

"Okay. I think some things were, well, put here to protect. Sort of like antibodies.

42

Other things are here to destroy. Like germs. That's about all I've got."

"Now you're starting to sound like a '50s monster movie."

But he was also starting to make some sense.

"John!"

"Yeah, Patty?"

"Come in here please. Mac needs you."

Yeah, right.

"You'd better hang out here. I've never seen Mac after she's barfed before. It's probably not safe."

"No problem!"

When I got into Mac's office Patty closed the door behind me. Mac looked her usual self.

Which meant she looked pissed.

"Captain Martin, am I correct in my understanding that you can 'see' crimes that have already happened?" SISSI-boy and his suit looked none the worse for blowing lunch.

"Yeah. Like a rerun."

"Inspector MacDonald, I'm commandeering Captain Martin until further notice."

He shot a glance at my perfect partner Patty.

"And Detective O'Rourke, as well."

"Like hell you are!" Mac was standing now.

Not a good sign.

SISSI-boy's reply was cut off by Mac's phone ringing.

Freddy and Mac traded eye-daggers for three rings before I picked up the phone.

"MacDonald's Office, Martin speaking."

I listened. When the voice stopped, I handed the phone to Mac.

She put the phone to her ear, keeping her

eyes on Herbert.

"MacDonald."

Mac's eyes got wide.

Then her face went pale.

After twelve seconds she put the phone down.

Did I mention that Mac is most dangerous when she whispers?

"Be sure I get them back in one piece." Mac dropped her chin and peered at Freddy over her glasses, "No phone call will help you if I don't."

"That is my intention, Ma'am." Herbert touched the brim of his hat as he tilted his head to the right slightly.

I stared at SISSI-boy. I really wanted to wipe that half grin off his face with a solid right cross.

Go figure, me being protective of Mac.

"Captain Martin, you and your partner will come with me. We'll meet Agent Holloway at Grand Central Terminal."

"Agent Holloway?"

"FBI agent Napoleon Holloway. He and his partner, Agent Johnson, along with you and yours will make up my team. Understood?"

Holloway.

Napoleon Holloway.

Po.

Damn!

"Oh, that professor and your coroner will be joining us, too."

"Lisa? Why?"

"Because I think she's hot."

I didn't think about it.

It was sort of a reflex action.

I bent over and offered the SISSI-boy a hand up. I'll have to admit, I was a little surprised he was still conscious.

"What the hell was that for?"

"You didn't do your homework, did you?" Patty brushed past me to examine Freddy's jaw.

"Doctor Martin is John's ex. As in wife."

"Damn! Sorry Martin! I was just joking. Trying to break the tension…"

"John, you must learn how to control yourself."

"Yeah, I'll work on that Patty."

I fought the need to rub my right fist.

It hurt.

We gathered the Professor and went to pick up Lisa at Grand Central.

We breezed through the TSA checkpoints at Grand Central. Being attached to a Federal Agent sort of streamlines such things. Even so, the crowd was pretty thick.

I scanned the newspapers scattered throughout the huddled masses. No headlines about skyfish, rods, bloodthirsty killers, or demons.

Being six feet five inches tall has its advantages.

I looked over the crowd and spotted him.

His shoulders stood a foot above the waves of rolling heads.

"John? John Martin!" The crowd between us began to part. Like a ripple from the big man's movements. "Well, what-do-ya-know! John Martin!" Snake venom came out with more kindness.

A hand the size of Kansas grabbed each of my shoulders.

"Nice to see you, Po."

I lied.

"You do look a LOT worse for wear, John!" Po took a step back and ran his eyes up and down Patty. "And who is this angel?" A huge left hand lifted Po's fedora off of his head, the right one daintily outstretched in Patty's direction.

"Po, Patty. Patty, Po."

"Holloway, where's Johnson?"

"Hospital. Shingles."

"We'll do without her. Let's get a move on here. We still have to find Doctor Martin."

All business, that Freddy.

"John? I'd heard, I mean, I thought…" Po looked at me like I had two heads. He didn't let go of Patty's hand though.

"It's SISSI-boy's idea." I jerked a thumb at Freddy.

"John!" Patty gave me her best 'behave' look.

"Ha-ha-ha! Same old John! Always leaping before he looks." Po's laughter boomed over the crowd before he leaned close to squint at me, "That can be dangerous, you know." Po aimed his squint at Freddy, "SISSI-boy. I like that!"

Freddy just rolled his eyes and shook his head.

"Napoleon? Napoleon Holloway! Get over here, you monster!" Lisa was standing on a bench waving.

The green monster rose up again, but experience beat it down. First off, I knew Lisa and Po were friends and nothing more. Second, if I slugged Po like I had Freddy, he'd break me in half.

He'd done it before.

And once is more than enough.

I've always been a quick learner.

"Well, well, well! First an Angel, then Lisa and John Martin together again! This day keeps getting better and better!

"Nice to see you Po. And no, we are not together." Lisa's eyes fired a dagger at Patty. "As for the angel, I've not seen any wings."

"This way to the train. Let's get a move on, people." Freddy waved for us to follow.

"Agent Holloway," Patty wrapped her arms around Po's bicep. Well, halfway around. "Please tell me how you know Captain Martin."

"Well, John and I were on the trail of this killer. You see, he used to be my partner, before I went to the FBI. Anyway…"

A long day.

Yeah.

And getting longer by the minute.

4

I didn't try to sleep on the trip to D.C.
I was too busy arguing with SISSI-boy. Or
rather, arguing at him. I don't think he
heard a word I said…

"… and I still don't understand why we are
leaving a crime scene, three crime scenes,
with something this big unresolved…"

"Because we've been ordered to D.C."

"… and bringing Dr. Martin is totally
unnecessary…"

"Because we've been ordered to D.C."

"… and with the leads we have, the start
on the investigation…"

"Because we've been ordered to D.C."

"…and we could…"

"JOHN! Stop it."

Patty was different.

Not white-winged different.

Different like a big yellow Lab is when
protecting her young.

I shut up and stared at her.

"Well, I think it's exciting. We must be
going to D.C. to pick this up on a larger
scale." Wattson stared out the window of the
train as he spoke.

"Good deduction, Wattson." Freddy grinned
a little. So did I. I was thinking that he
might be human after all.

Lisa was standing next to Patty, glaring
down like a fury having a bad hair day.

Patty arched her back slightly and
stretched her arms up over her head.

You could hear every guy on the train
moan.

She followed her arms up and stood smiling
down at Lisa.

"I'm going to make Agent Holloway tell me the rest of that story. The parts he said were not for mixed company."

Lisa sat down next to me. "You never told her about Cleo, did you?"

"Why should I? I'm not too happy with the way that turned out."

"Cleo who?"

Lisa gave Freddy her 'mind your own beeswax' look.

"Cleo Holloway? You were in on that?" I thought Wattson was going to drool all over Freddy.

"Go ahead, tell them." In the face of overwhelming firepower, total surrender was my only option.

Lisa never gave me the chance.

"Po, c'mon back here will you?"

Lisa's revenge, take 4,397.

"He tells it so much better than I do."

She sat back, folding her arms in satisfaction.

I kept looking for smoke to come out of her ears…

"I really do have to thank you for this some time."

Yeah, I still remembered that 'married whisper.'

"Hey, darlin' Lisa. Everything okay here?"

"Yes Po. Thanks for asking. These nice people want to know about Cleo."

Patty materialized behind my former partner. I gave her my best 'HELP!' look.

She only stared blankly back at me in reply.

Po sat down.

I'm not sure the guy that was in that seat left first.

49

"John and I were after this killer. Nasty guy. Chopped people up in front of their friends, kids, parents. Got off on the audience."

"Po, you don't have to…"

He ignored me.

"We had tracked him into this Harlem nightclub. Just so happens Cleopatra was singing there that night."

"Po…"

His lip quivered. I saw a tear well up in his left eye.

All these years he never cried, screamed, nothing.

Except that night.

"Shut up, John. Cleopatra was born Cleopatra Holloway. She was my little sister."

Napoleon looked soft, kind of melted like.

"Somebody set off the fire alarm. Then I blacked out.

"When I came to, Cleo was tied up on the stage. I was tied to a chair watching. The guy…he…cut…"

"Po, don't."

He gave me a look.

"He made me watch while he cut her up. Fingers first. Then her toes. Hands, arms, legs. She was gone before he finished."

"John came in and the guy ran out. He chased him, but didn't catch him. If he…"

"If I had just come back sooner, she'd be alive."

I didn't think anyone could hear me.

"I'm sorry, John. I shouldn't have done what I did."

"You mean almost kill me? I was screening the crowd outside. I didn't know. The doors were locked, I couldn't get back in. If I

50

had… When I couldn't catch the guy, I came back in and untied Po. He started…it took me a month to recover."

"You only see what has happened, not what will happen. I know. I'm…John, I'm sorry."

Damn.

What could I say?

"Forget-about-it."

Her lips hit my cheek as Patty's lips hit the top of Po's head.

For that split second, all was right in the world.

Then the train made an emergency stop.

And I woke up.

Po looked like he wanted to start beating on me all over again.

Except…

He was looking past me.

And his hands were in the air.

Damn.

A loud crack sounded behind my left ear. Then another. The smell of gunpowder gagged me.

Freddie fell into the floor in front of me. Most of his head was gone.

Po backed up. Not making eye contact with me, he blinked twice.

It was an old signal between us. Big trouble.

I saw the red stain spreading on his shoulder.

Damn.

I noticed Wattson and Lisa behind him. I couldn't see Patty.

I usually try to avoid sitting slumped over, mouth open, and a string of drool hanging down while I'm in public. Right now I was glad I hadn't moved.

51

I saw the shoes. Two pair.

My right hand was hanging next to my right calf.

My fingers inched up my pant leg…

Got it.

I swung the blade up into the second guy's crotch. His scream did the rest.

The first guy turned his head. That's when Po's hands came down.

Crumpled.

It's strange seeing a person crumple like an empty beer can at a frat party.

I kept the blade in the second guy as I lifted up.

It stopped cutting near his right kidney.

I looked at where the knife went into the guy's back.

Blood and wires.

Wires?

I slid the blade out slowly then lifted the guy's jacket.

I'd sliced through the wires between the batteries and the explosives taped around the guy.

Terrorists.

Lisa was trying to get at Po's shoulder.

I heard shouting from behind me.

Po shoved Lisa to the ground. Wattson bent over to help her.

I looked back just in time to see the explosion.

Loud.

Like inside thunder loud.

Bright white, then yellow and orange.

Then black smoke.

My eyes burned.

Something sliced my left ear. Something else hit me hard outside my right eye.

52

Another something bounced hard off my left shoulder.

Something big pulled the air past my face.

It took my brain about three seconds to register the pain. Things were moving...slow.

Funny.

I saw the smoke part as Patty emerged, blackened, scraped and torn. She had two kids, one under each arm.

Limp.

Pale.

Her eyes were wet.

About to burst.

Lisa was there.

She can move pretty fast.

She did her doctor thing. Feeling, looking, listening.

Lisa lifted her head like she was looking at Patty. All I could see was her head move side to side once.

Damn.

Patty's eyes closed. Her head hung down.

I swear I saw a light come over her and the kids. Like a blanket, protecting...

Patty's face relaxed and the whole train car brightened. One tear ran down her face, but she smiled. For a second I thought I saw the wings again.

All this happened in the three seconds before Po's body hit the ground.

"LISA!"

I'm told that my voice can get sorta loud and commanding at times.

She was over him in a flash, moving frantically.

She ripped his bloody, shredded jacket and shirt open, and then she just froze.

I wish I'd never looked over her shoulder.

The hole in Po's chest was wide and deep. No blood. That was spreading out beneath him. Whatever had hit him had shredded his heart. I looked at his face...

His eyes moved to look at me. A huge hand grabbed my collar. His lips moved.

I think he said "Sorry."

Could be wishful thinking.

Damn.

I looked around the car.

I needed something to crush, something I could give pain to.

Something I could kill.

I ripped the explosives off of the body of the guy I'd stabbed and tossed them out the window.

Patty had wet eyes again.

Wattson sat down in a seat, pale from the shock.

Lisa had me in her arms. I felt her lips on my forehead.

I looked around what was left of the train again.

King Kong would have been in for a world of hurt if he showed up then.

These three were mine to protect now.

"Hold still." Lisa was cleaning the cut on my ear. Why she had stitches with her, I'll never know, but she sewed my ear up. And my eye.

Patty was next to Po's body. Her eyes closed, head bowed. She turned to me.

"He's sorry."

"Yeah, me too." I gulped it out.

Barely.

Po was a good partner, a sweet guy.

Patty reached her hand out, touching Lisa's shoulder, then mine. I felt better.

Things started moving normally for me then.

Lisa looked like she'd shed a big burden. Patty moved towards Wattson.

"Sweet Jesus!"

All eyes went to Wattson. His eyes looked as if they'd pop out of his head and fly out the window.

I followed his gaze to the pasture outside the train.

It wasn't green.

Not anymore.

A dozen cattle lay near the tracks. Another dozen were strewn across the pasture.

Well, parts of the cattle.

"Patty, head to the back of the train. See if there's anything we need to act on back there. Or if there's anyone we can help. Wattson, stay here with Lisa." I gave my ex the best Police Captain stare I could. "You stay here. If there are survivors, we'll bring them to you. Here."

I moved towards the front of the train.

There weren't any passengers forward of us.

No one rides the trains these days.

One of the terrorists sat on the floor just outside the driver's cockpit, his back to me. He clutched the trigger in his hand, sobbing, "The Devil! I looked at Satan. I'm damned," over and over while he rocked back and forth.

I was happy to fulfill his personal prophecy.

I grabbed the trigger in one hand and shoved the other up from underneath his chin.

The loud snap and the limpness of his body came at the same time.

I kept the trigger in my hand as I rolled him onto his back and cut the wires to the

batteries. You don't cut the trigger wires-
they could short across the knife blade and
detonate the bomb.

I kicked out the closest emergency exit
window and tossed the explosive belt out.

It came back and slammed into my face.

I still had the trigger in my hand.

I finally managed to ditch the explosives.
I got a split lip for my troubles. Could have
been worse, I suppose.

The train operator was dead, his hand on
the emergency stop. The guy must have known
he'd be killed, but he kept them from blowing
up Union Station.

I went back through the wreckage to check
on Lisa, Wattson, and Patty.

Lisa and Wattson were gone.

So much for my best Police Captain's
stare.

I moved further back. Patty had found some
survivors in the very rear of the train. It
looked like there had been a lot of fire back
there, but either it had burned out by the
time Patty got there, or…

Patty told me she'd tried bringing them up
to Lisa, but she had to bring Lisa back to
them. Wattson came along and gave credible
help treating the wounded.

Some passengers began calling Patty The
Amtrak Angel.

Go figure.

I started looking around the pasture.

The cow parts reminded me of the
schoolyard.

Like I needed that.

I was having a tough time sorting out
everything with Po. It was one thing to have
your best friend blame you for his sister's
death.

56

It was something else to have him dead.
Like, gone.
Forever.
Damn.
"Do you want to talk about it?"
Lisa's hand on my shoulder helped.
"I don't know what to say."
"Just tell me what you feel."
So I did.
About Po.
About the schoolyard.
About…
She listened.
It helped.
Pretty soon the locals came. Then the FBI, then the NSA. I turned into a kind of alphabet soup pretty quickly after that.

"John Martin?" The squeaky little voice calling my name belonged to a barely five foot tall suit under a tight bun of bright orange hair.

I could feel the daggers from Lisa's eyes landing all over my back.

"Yes?"

"Director Samantha Marlowe, SISSI. Call me Sam. Follow me please." She turned and started walking without a glance back. How something so small could project so much authority…

I shouted for Patty, Wattson, and Lisa to follow me.

Then I followed Sam.

I lost her in a group of black SUVs. Pretty clichéd, but that's what it was.

"Over here, Captain Martin."

We piled into the white HUMVEE idling behind the black SUVs. Sam was behind the wheel.

I helped Lisa climb up into the HUMVEE. Wattson helped Patty.

"Seatbelts are mandatory," Sam squeaked from the driver's seat. I couldn't help but wonder how her feet could reach the pedals. I stopped wondering when she floored the armored HUMVEE and we sped off in a cloud of burning rubber.

I had never expected to see the insides of an underground bunker.

But in twenty minutes that's where I was.

Thing was, I didn't care.

I was exhausted.

Drained.

I needed sleep.

And Scotch.

And something…more…

"This way, Captain Martin." Sam's hard soled shoes echoed down the hallway.

I followed.

She stopped and opened a door.

I went in.

I saw the cot.

I collapsed.

Sometime later, my aching back kicked me out of the cot. I took the opportunity to see what else was in the room.

Another cot.

Someone under the covers, back to me.

Long, shining brown hair hung down...

Lisa.

She stirred and rolled over. She stretched her arms and her eyes flickered open.

She smiled.

She was naked under the blanket.

I knew because she wasn't all under the blanket anymore.

Damn!

58

She smiled, lounging on her side, propped up on one elbow.

"You still snore."

I swallowed.

I don't know how Rhode Island got in my throat.

"Are you sure this is a good idea?"

Lisa sat up and tilted her head. The blanket fell to the floor.

Damn.

"We're in the same room, John. Not the same bed."

"Damn."

She laughed.

I smiled.

Usually at this point I'd say something really stupid.

This time I stayed quiet.

Good move.

"I'm sorry, John."

I swallowed something.

I think it was Connecticut.

"Lisa, I…"

"No, don't. You'll say something stupid and piss me off. Just listen."

I nodded like a bobble-head.

I felt like a bobble-head.

She'd always had that effect on me.

Life had taught me a lot of things. One of them is to never expect the best outcome.

So I waited for her to tell me I owed her more alimony.

"I should have believed you about Patty. And Cleo. I, I wasn't fair to you."

"Lisa…"

She was sitting next to me.

"SHUSH! Just let me say this. It's not

easy, you know."

Her finger sealed my lips…

I did the bobble-head thing again.

Hey, if it's working, why change it?

"I still…can we start…Aw, shit!"

She was over me. Her mouth was on mine. Her tongue…she remembered…things…

As suddenly as it started it ended.

Lisa was back on her cot, face as red as Moscow on May Day.

Damn.

"John, I, I'm sorry."

She began sobbing into her hands.

Damn. Damn. DAMN!

I was next to her, my arm around her.

She melted into the familiar position.

"Let's just take this slow, okay? I think it's important enough not to screw it up this time."

Did I say that?

Part of me, a big, growing part of me, did not want to take this slow.

Not at all.

She looked up at me.

I liked that look in her eyes.

We sat together, quiet, for a long time. That was fine with me. I remember thinking that I was getting old, enjoying 'cuddling' so much…

The knock on the door pulled me out of the enjoyment.

"Damn."

"John."

"Yeah, I know. I was hoping everything up until a few minutes ago was a bad dream."

"Somehow you're important in this. You and Patty."

I looked at Lisa. No sneer or venom when

she said that name.

"Am I really awake?"

She slugged my arm.

"Go on!"

I stood up. Stretched. Sniffed...

"I need a shower."

"You have twenty five minutes!" Sam's voice came through the door.

I looked at Lisa.

Her eyes sparkled.

She smiled.

Hot damn!

Thirty five minutes later, we were getting an abbreviated tour of the bunker.

For the first time since the alley, I wasn't thinking of my next bottle of Scotch.

All I remember of the tour is that everything was grey.

Grey walls.

Grey ceiling.

Grey floor.

Grey doors.

Grey furniture.

I know how the government works.

Grey paint must be cheap.

We all ended up in a large conference room. Big enough for around thirty people, I figured.

Then I counted.

Okay, it was big enough for forty five people.

Sam took center stage.

I had figured out enough to expect that by now.

Hey, I *am* a detective.

"Ladies and Gentlemen. We are here to organize a response to the unusual… attacks, which we have suffered lately. We have assembled you all here, a variety of exceptional talents, to aid our efforts."

I took a look around. Not a soul I recognized. But, hey, it's a big country.

"The best information we have so far has been provided by Captain John Martin, NYPD, his partner, Lieutenant Patricia Margaret Theresa O'Rourke, Doctor Lisa Martin, MD, ME, and Professor Albert Wattson, MS, PhD. Dr. Wattson, if you would, please."

Albert? All this time and we never asked him his first name.

"Thank you, eh, Director Marlowe. Ah-hem. Well, the most efficient way to convey this information is to show you all. So…" Wattson hit a button and the room darkened.

A screen lit up.

I recognized the scene.

It was the middle school.

I turned away.

Thankfully there was no sound.

I still heard those screams.

"What we have here is a…well, let's just say that many legends about demons, gargoyles, and devils could have sprung from something like this. The behavior isn't just feeding, it is…"

Wattson paused for several seconds. I looked up. He was swallowing hard.

"It is about more than that. It's about inflicting pain and instilling terror.

"There are some other events worth noting. I have nothing concrete, but I believe these events are connected."

The alley came up on the screen. The knife attack on the woman, and the 'nothing' attack on the perp.

I noticed a buzz ripple through the room.

"These recordings were made in an…unusual way, thanks to Captain Martin. I can verify they are authentic. These things did happen. No special effects, no trick photography, blue screens, green screens, or CG. These events did happen.

"I believe something is happening, something that, based upon a variety of sources, from fossils to legends and myths, happens every five thousand years or so. And, it's happening again now."

"Thank you, Dr. Wattson. Now, we know that this creature, or creatures, has attacked several schools, livestock, and sporting events across the country. I have reports that these attacks have happened in Asia, Europe, Africa, and Australia. Our job is to stop these attacks.

"For this task, we have assembled all of you here. You have been assigned to teams of four. These assignments are in the envelopes you've been given. Break into your teams and report as indicated on your cards. That is all."

I turned to Lisa and Patty. "I didn't get any envelo…"

"Captain Martin, this is for you."

Sam was right in front of me, waving an envelope in my face. I could see she had three more.

I took mine, and Sam handed another to Patty, one to Lisa, and one to Wattson.

I looked at my envelope. The only thing on it was my name.

I opened it and took out a card made of heavy paper stock.

It was blank except for the number 1.

"Will you all please line up according to the number on your card. Number one nearest the door, please." Sam had a way of making her tiny voice heard over the rumble of the crowd around us.

I stood at the door, looking around. Patty, Wattson, and Lisa.

One big happy family, we were.

I was still trying to sort out what had happened with Lisa. I stole a glance at her. She smiled.

So, it wasn't a dream.

I expected to confront one of these demon-things before too much longer.

Or a crazy killer with pale skin, long teeth and anti-coagulating saliva.

Or both.

And Lisa would be with me.

Damn.

"Hey, why so dark all of a sudden?"

Her voice was small and scared. Her hand on my cheek was pleading…

I kissed her. Hard. She kissed back.

"Break it up, children."

How Sam's squeaky little voice could boom around the auditorium is beyond me.

Lisa looked into my eyes.

"You're worried about protecting me!"

She grabbed my head and pulled me into another kiss.

I'm no dummy.

I didn't resist.

Lisa pulled back before Sam could comment.

We were ushered out of the auditorium and down a long hallway.

Just the four of us.

Down an elevator, along a corridor past two armed guards in black fatigues, combat armor and helmets. We finally stopped outside of a heavy door.

Sam waved her ID at the door and it

opened.

We were in an armory.

"Ladies and gentlemen, this is the SISSI Armory. Highly efficient weapons of every type. Please take some time to browse around. You have twelve minutes to select your weapons."

Something shiny caught my eye. It reminded me that my own Colt 45 was not nestled into that comforting nook inside my jacket. They took it when we arrived here.

I picked up what looked like my Colt, boxy and heavy, but was nearly twice the size and half the weight.

It was tethered to a canvas backpack.

I looked over the business end of the thing. No muzzle. Just a shiny, clear lens…

"That is a Mark 34 electron accelerator. It fires ultra-high velocity electron pulses at microsecond intervals. The effect is like a beam of pure electricity."

"A lightning bolt gun!"

I glanced at Patty. She had some sort of contraption that looked like a rifle.

Sort of.

"Ah, the Mark 3 77-caliber Browning Automatic Rocket Rifle. Each round is a programmable rocket. Zero recoil, maximum effect over a two mile range."

Wattson was standing in the middle of the room just looking lost.

"Doctor Wattson, allow me to make some suggestions for you…" Sam pulled the confused man over to a wall near the rear of the Armory.

"I'm ready!" Lisa popped up in front of me. I looked at her hands.

Nothing.

I frowned at her face.

"At least get a decent handgun. You're a good shot. At least, you used to be…"

"Shush. I'll be fine. I've got my weapon right here," she patted her chest, right between those…

I shook my head.

"What, is love going to protect you?"

The last thing I needed was to lose her now because she'd turned into a schoolgirl with a crush.

"Ha-ha. Of course it will, silly," she grinned as she reached into her blouse and pulled out a thin, three inch long tube with a pistol grip.

"Aahh! Mrs. Martin has chosen well," Sam grinned as she looked at me.

"This is the DG 50 needler. It fires a half millimeter diameter dart using a magnetic charge. The dart is made of crystallized cyanide along a magnetic core. It travels at 3,000 feet per second, enough velocity to penetrate a Kevlar vest. Once it enters a body, it dissolves into a poison that blocks the body's ability to use oxygen."

"As long as these gargoyle things use oxygen."

Sam gave me a sour look and went back to helping Wattson.

"John, what do you think?" Patty had the rifle slung across her back and a long knife scabbard on her belt. Right next to the shiny chromed Colt 45…

"Oh, no you don't! Fork it over."

Patty laughed and handed me the holster.

I gave it to Lisa.

"You know how to use this. That thing, I don't know about,"

I grabbed the needler and handed to Patty.

"In case something gets past your BAR."

"You mean, BARR."

"Too many war movies as a kid. It's a BAR."

Patty looked at the tiny thing, and stuffed it into her…

Did I mention that Patty never wore a bra?

"This will do rather nicely, I expect," Wattson walked over to us holding what appeared to be a teched-up six shooter. There was a cord attached, running up his sleeve to a backpack a lot like mine, but smaller.

"It's a pulse laser. The laser pulses from one chamber, then it rotates and fires the next. Meanwhile, the other one recharges. By the time the first chamber is in firing position again, it's fully charged."

I looked over the three of them.

Patty I didn't worry about.

Wattson had enough sense to run first and fire only as a last resort.

Lisa could hold her own against a Marine platoon with the Colt.

But…

Something was missing.

I looked at Patty's waist again.

I smiled.

I walked behind a partition. It only took a second to pick them out.

"Here. The bottom strap goes around your thigh. Not too loose, you don't want it flapping if you have to run. Not too tight, either, or you won't be able to run."

I passed out the Bowie knives to Lisa and Wattson. Each had a nine inch blade. Big enough to be effective, but not too big for them to handle.

Mine was a little bigger.

"John, a sword, really?"

"It's a Dirk, Hon. Only half the size of a sword," I explained as I strapped the scabbard to my thigh. "The blade's only twenty inches."

When we had finished strapping on our gear Sam led us to a firing range.

Wattson almost burned the bunker down. The Professor couldn't hit the target.

Patty got the hang of the BAR quickly. She dead centered the bull's-eye from a kilometer.

Lisa took four shots with the Colt. All bull's-eyes.

She'd been practicing.

It took me a few shots to get used to the lightening rifle. It had a pretty strong kick-back.

The third shot burned the bull's-eye.

We practiced some more, getting the feel of our weapons. Wattson was a quick learner, and got to where he was a reasonable shot.

Little did we know these toys wouldn't help us.

Not one bit.

5

We were assigned to find the source of the 'disturbances' in the Northeastern U.S. Sam gave us a Marine recon platoon as support. It made me wonder what we were in for.

Tracking scum through the five boroughs is one thing. Tracking, then fighting demons and vampires is something else. The murderers and rapists we usually hunted were generally cowards at heart.

This was entirely different.

And it was all my fault.

My fault because at the intelligence briefing I spoke up and said the Yonkers location was the most likely location for a headquarters.

Like I could see them, all together, planning…

So that's where we headed.

It was my fault because if I had not looked to find out what happened to that perp in the alley, Po would still be alive. And Wattson would be juggling test tubes. And Patty would be stopping traffic.

And Lisa would be safely in the morgue instead of flying towards the demon's lair.

Damn.

It hit me then. She was the first priority. I'd sacrifice all the others for her safety. Everyone. Everywhere.

And myself.

It took me a while to figure that out.

It took longer to come to grips with it.

I'd always thought of myself as a stand-up kind of guy, on the side of 'good' and all that. Willing to do the 'right' thing, even if it meant sacrificing, well, me.

I had a tough time with that once I knew I'd chuck everything to protect Lisa.

Then our plane banked hard to the right. Or starboard. Whatever.

Something hit the plane hard.

I saw a flash of red through the window.

I looked for Lisa.

Fear welled up in her eyes.

Eyes pleading with me to make it all right.

The plane banked left. Hard.

I glanced out the window again.

Trees.

Above us.

I grabbed her.

We hit the ground hard.

It was loud and fast.

A leaf was in my mouth.

Blood was on my shirt.

I had Lisa in my arms.

Was this her blood?

Damn!

We stopped. The Marines were everywhere, guns ready, covering every direction.

It didn't matter.

I saw a flash of a red, scaly something in front of me.

Guns fired.

The four Marines nearest me vanished.

A boot fell in front of me.

Another red flash.

More gunfire.

Lisa was gone.

I screamed.

"DAMN!"

Patty flew past me.

She was…

Different.

I'd seen them before.

Just a glimpse.

Wings.

Big, white, wings.

I was on my feet, after her. But Patty went up.

Way up.

Then I saw it.

It had to be thirty feet long, at least five times Lisa's length.

It had her in its hand, so I could tell.

Patty was on its back. Whatever she was doing, the demon, gargoyle, or devil didn't like it.

I lifted my rifle.

Patty was in my line of fire.

And Lisa.

Patty drove the thing lower. As they came closer, I could see what she was doing.

She was tearing great chunks of flesh out of the thing, with her hands and teeth.

Big teeth.

The demon screamed, and screamed again.

And dropped Lisa.

I dropped the rifle and ran as fast as I could.

I wasn't going to make it.

Not even close.

As Lisa fell, her eyes held mine.

My heart screamed.

I couldn't watch.

I couldn't look away.

Down she fell.

Ten meters.

Five.

Faster than you can tell it, she fell.

I ran as fast as I could, but I knew I couldn't save her.

A foot from the ground, Patty caught her.

Patty set Lisa down next to me.

Then the demon swallowed Patty.

I grabbed Lisa and I screamed curses at the thing. I cursed as I had never cursed before.

Wattson fired his laser and somehow hit the thing. Six marines fired at it too.

I think they pissed it off.

I drew my sword.

The mouth came for me.

And Lisa.

Big enough to shoot pool in.

I dove in.

It may not have been the smart move, at least not in that thing's mind.

If it had one.

I really wished I had one of those six foot long broadswords.

Or a lance.

I pushed the dirk I did have out in front of me, shoving it up as hard as I could while I shoved my feet down against the thing's tongue. It was in to the hilt.

The thing's mouth smelled like week old sushi in a horse barn.

Teeth went into my right calf.

Then they let go.

I fell about ten feet.

It felt like ten miles.

I landed on my ass.

Hard.

The thing fell on top of me.

I remember my right leg hurting like hell.

Then everything went black.

Wattson told me later that Patty came out through the thing's chest just as I dove in.

So much for getting that cool monster-slayer tattoo.

I woke up to Lisa's face.

I smiled.

Then my right leg reminded me that it hurt like hell.

"Shh…the pain meds should kick in soon. I had to…"

I sat up and looked at my leg.

No shoe.

Just a huge lump of white bandages, stained with red…

I fell back down.

Hard.

Dizzy.

"John, be still. You've lost a lot of blood. I had to stitch your leg up. It's just temporary, until you get to a hospital. You'll be fine."

Something warm and wet touched my forehead. Her hair covered my head.

Her smell covered my pain.

Jasmine.

The pain was gone. Lisa's bedside manner or the Marine's morphine, I didn't know.

I didn't care.

Well, that's not entirely accurate.

I do know that I slept for a long time.

I know because I remember the dreams.

Nightmares.

Demons, gargoyles, devils.

Everywhere.

Killing, eating almost everyone.

Vampires running after the rest.

Damn.

One was after Lisa.

I killed it.

Three more were after her.

Then nine.

I had to kill them all.

There were too many.

One got to her.

"NO!" I screamed.

And I sat up.

My leg did a fine job of reminding me that sudden movements were not a good idea.

I swear it took the hospital staff a full ten seconds to stop staring at me and get back to work.

The first thing that hit me was how cold I was.

The second was that Lisa was holding one hand, and Patty the other.

Wattson and Sam were standing at the foot of the bed.

"Sorry. Bad dream."

"I don't doubt it, Captain Martin." Sam sounded like she was commenting on the weather report. "Really, diving into the mouth of the beast?"

"I should have taken a bigger sword."

Everyone laughed.

Even me.

Then I looked at Sam.

"How long?"

"Two days."

"Any other attacks?"

"No. I think they're in shock."

"They're in shock?"

Like, I'm not?

"They think? They plan? They retreat? How do…"

Patty cut me off.

"John, they think you killed it."

"I didn't? Who did?"

Wattson brought an iPad up to me and started a video.

I watched as the thing swallowed Patty and then turned towards Lisa. I saw my feeble leap into the mouth. It had felt like a ten foot jump. It looked like about a foot. I saw the sword's tip stick up out of the top of the thing's snout, far from anything vital. I saw Patty rip her way out of the thing's belly.

Then I saw chunks of the thing disappear. Not more than three seconds, and it was gone. All of it.

"Rods."

"Damn!"

"John Martin!"

"Sorry, Patty. Please forgive me, Father!"

"That's better. John, they think you killed the demon. They don't know about me. That is important."

"Know about you… Patty, that… you're…"

Her wings spread out. All white and glowing and…

Angelic.

"It must be the pain meds."

Lisa squeezed my hand.

"No, John. She's the real deal."

"It is what I am, John."

"Scientifically verified, John."

"Captain Martin, it would seem that we are in the middle of a recurring conflict between good and evil."

"Sam's right, John. Every five thousand years the battle loses all semblances of civility, subtlety, and nuance. It degrades into a knockdown, drag-out brawl. That's why we're here, why I'm here. It's sooner than expected, but it's real."

"Damn!"

"John Martin!"

"I'm sorry. Forgive me Father. So, Sam, what's next?"

"You get better."

"Thanks for the get-well-soon wishes. But what nex…"

"John, you get well before we do anything else."

I stared at Sam for a few seconds.

I didn't like what I was hearing.

"Why?"

"Because you can see them."

"I see what has already happened…"

"You can see what they're planning if you know where they are and you concentrate. That's why they're after you."

I didn't like what Patty was saying.

"After ME?"

"Try it."

I closed my eyes at Sam's challenge.

The hospital room faded out, replaced by a dim cavern.

A group of about a dozen horrors sat in a circle. The big one turned his head and looked straight at me…

"Yes, after you. Think about it. Everything…" Sam's voice pulled me back to the hospital room.

I thought about it.

"Lisa, you're going someplace safe."

It was my best 'no arguments, just do it!' voice.

And I knew it wouldn't work.

"Like hell…" Lisa swallowed hard and glanced at the frowning Patty, "I am doing no such thing, John Paul Martin!"

Damn.

"We will have a briefing on our next move tomorrow at 9 AM. Until then, rest and recuperate, Captain Martin. Oh, and may I add, well done!"

"What does a guy have to do to get a decent steak around here, anyway?"

Wattson laughed.

I was really starting to like the guy.

Patty smiled.

Lisa got up and went to the nurses' station.

Sam smiled and left.

My leg began to throb…

"Nurse!"

Patty laid her hand on my leg.

The pain vanished.

Patty looked pale for a moment, and then her glow returned.

"Patty, that, that hurt you, didn't it."

"I'll have no such talk, partner."

Her voice cracked just a bit.

"Please, don't. It, it's not right for you to take that for me."

The nurse was fussing with the IV pump.

She smiled, "John, don't you remember?" My eyes wouldn't stay open. Patty's voice sounded like she was down a long hallway… "I'm only following His example…"

I woke up early the next morning, around 3 AM I think. Lisa was snoring, Patty was sitting with her eyes closed, and Wattson was asleep, drool crawling down his cheek.

That impressed me.

Not the drool.

Wattson didn't have to be there.

But he was.

I took the time to take inventory of the situation.

My Partner was an angel.

The Professor was a stand-up guy.

My ex still loved me.

And demons were trying to erase all that.

And everything else.

It made me angry.

Not in the 'I'll kick your face in' way, but more like, 'Oh, you want to take this? REALLY? I don't think so!' kind of way, if that makes any sense.

So I used the time to think.

About a lot of things.

Then Patty asked, "Are you all right, John?"

"I don't know. This is a lot to digest."

"In some ways it is. But from another point of view, you and I are just on another case."

What she said made some sense. I thought about it for a while. I felt better.

Patty and I had solved over two hundred cases. As I looked back, we had a 100% conviction rate.

We were good.

Damn good.

Now this was dumped on us.

All of a sudden, I felt like I could take on Hell itself and win.

And that was exactly what we were doing.

My eyes wondered over to Lisa's sleeping form.

She was so pretty, so peaceful, so vulnerable…

Damn!

"Patty, is…are…should I…do we…"

"That question is above my pay-grade, John

Martin. Just know that happiness is where we find it."

I sat up and looked around the room, scanning for danger.

"John, you're safe here. She's safe here. Relax."

"I can't. If she's in danger…"

"Learn to deal with it. All people are in danger all the time. You worry about…the demons hurting her. Let me tell you that they will not do that."

I took a big breath in and let it out slowly.

This was quite a revelation.

I sat up a little taller.

Could Patty see the future, the outcome of all of this?

"No, John. All I know is that this Evil will not harm her as long as you are alive. That does not mean it will not try to…"

"Patty, I don't understand."

"John, keep your wits about you. Don't take wild chances. Be smart, like the partner I've known. That will keep her safe."

So, I thought about that for a while.

Really, really hard.

I needed to use my training.

Go figure!

"Patty, what is your role in all of this?"

"All I know is that I'm here to help fight them."

"The Rods?"

"Another weapon in the battle."

"Do I need to…"

"No. They will not harm the innocent. Remember the children and the chocolate."

This was a lot to digest.

Especially with my leg throbbing.

The nurse responded to my call fairly quickly. She had the pain meds with her.

"What would you rate your pain as?"

"Unbearable."

"Mr. Martin, would you rate your pain on a scale from one to ten, ten being unbearable?"

"Three hundred and forty thousand, seven hundred and twelve."

"All right. Ten. This should help."

She pressed buttons on the IV pump.

The room started spinning.

"Ah, okay. How about 'seven'?"

I hate sleeping in a spinning room without enjoying getting drunk.

The room spun me into another sleep anyway.

The next thing I remember was Sam tugging at my ear.

"Mr. Martin! Are you ready for your briefing?"

I don't remember exactly what I tried to say, but what I heard come out sounded like, "Hal-mums bid everdab!"

"Good! Then we shall proceed."

To be honest, I have no clue what Sam said after that.

I do know it involved us going to Turkey.

Have I mentioned that I hate flying?

Damn.

I hate flying.

Yet there I was, the next day, 40,000 feet over the Atlantic Ocean.

Go figure.

Lisa was next to me.

So life was good.

My leg felt fine.

Most of the time.

Wattson and Patty sat in front of us. They

80

talked a lot. I couldn't hear what they were saying, but I could read their tones.

And the occasional perfect giggle.

It made me smile.

I looked at Lisa, asleep with her head on my shoulder.

I thought I'd give anything to just sit like this forever.

"…they're after you, John Martin!"

I sat up with a start.

I closed my eyes.

Red demons swarmed around the airliner. At least a dozen of them. Circling, spiraling, waiting…

"Patty! They're here, ready to attack this plane!"

Patty turned to look at me.

Her eyes burned.

Then she disappeared.

I grabbed my dirk.

I don't know what Patty did, what she went through. I do know the plane was never attacked.

I woke Lisa up. Patty would need her, I was sure.

A few minutes later, Patty was back. Her face was scratched, her clothing in tatters.

Covered in blood.

Lisa tended to her.

What part of medical school dealt with treating angels injured in combat with demons, I don't know. I do know that Lisa helped Patty.

And 24 hours ago, that never would have happened.

Yeah, it would have. Lisa would have just complained about it.

It was the middle of the night when the

plane landed at a NATO base in Turkey. The thought of walking on the tarmac in the dark made me nervous. I closed my eyes at the door.

Nothing.

The four of us climbed into a waiting black Landrover. As soon as the doors closed, the driver grunted, "Seatbelts!" and sped off, followed by six black HUMVEEs.

I knew the cavern I'd glimpsed was southeast of the airport, amid a high mountain range. Up past the permanent snowcap. We weren't wasting any time. We headed straight for it.

With a few surprises.

I knew that my dirk and Patty's teeth and claws hurt the last demon. I figured a couple of grenades exploding inside one would do sort of what the Rods did, shred it.

So I made each of us carry four.

Did I mention that grenades are heavy?

I figured it would take us the better part of a day to reach the caverns. Lisa was asleep. Patty was whispering to Wattson.

I leaned back and closed my eyes.

I saw the back of his head first as he leaned over the woman. Thin, colorless hair, shirt a dirty grey with dark stains. Most looked old and dried, but near his collar a stain glistened, wet and red.

He looked at me and grinned. The guy had pasty, pale skin that looked two sizes too small for his face. His teeth made no sense, like long thin needles.

Blood smeared his face and teeth. He licked his lips and stepped back, a showman's sweep of his arm pulling my gaze to the woman.

Lisa sat up, blood seeping out of the wound on her neck. She smiled at me, lips

82

pasty and pale, teeth, long and needle-like…

"John!" Lisa's head jerked off of my shoulder at Patty's call.

"They're taunting me. Trying to rattle me."

"Like that serial killer. The one who left us trails to follow."

"Yeah." Patty's mention of our first major case together put my mind back into Cop-Mode.

"The Gretel Killer case."

"What was the Gretel Killer case?"

"Really, Professor, you don't know?" Lisa seemed surprised.

"The Gretel Killer. Left a trail for us to follow, usually about a mile long before it just faded out. Used parts of the victim like Hansel and Gretel used breadcrumbs. She was quite the celebrity for two months or so. The first case I saw…"

"I don't usually read the paper or watch the news. Maybe I've been too engrossed in my research." Wattson turned to look at Patty.

The ride was uneventful after that. Other than being very bumpy.

We pulled to a stop about a quarter mile from the mouth of the caverns about mid-morning. The soldiers spread out around us as we made our way towards it.

Without a clue about what to do once we got there.

Bad idea.

The soldiers formed a perimeter around the mouth of the caverns, taking cover behind the tan rock outcroppings and grey boulders. I glanced up at the sky, the sun nearly blinding me.

Did I mention it gets really hot in the mountains of Turkey sometimes?

Even above the snowcap.

It was hotter than Hell right now.

But the snow wasn't melting…

Shielding my eyes with my hand, I scanned for the demons. I spotted it on the mountain's peak, just as it jumped into flight.

I had expected it to be graceful in the air. It wasn't. It jerked and sputtered, the long, scalloped wings flapping almost comically. Like a fish out of water, trying to walk. But it flew.

Then it dove.

Fast.

It was headed right for Lisa.

I never saw the missile, just the contrail that pointed to the fighter that fired it.

The demon exploded.

Small arms fire erupted from the soldiers, then I heard a loud "Waaaa-HOOSH!" as an anti-tank rocket was fired. I glanced at Lisa, then Patty and Wattson before looking at the cave.

Twenty or so grey-skinned things ran out of the cave seconds before the rocket hit the stone above the cave's mouth. Dust obscured everything, but I heard rocks fall. A lot of them.

Then the soldiers started screaming.

I watched a group of four Marines get overrun by three of the grey-skinned creatures. A bite, a scream, and then the vamps ran to the next group.

Then the soldiers I thought were dead stood up.

One looked at me. Hollow eyes set in a pale grey face.

Long, funny, needle-like teeth…

He began walking, then running towards me.

Damn.

84

A loud crack deafened my left ear.

The soldier's head exploded. The 45 will do that to ya.

Another crack, another exploded vampire head.

And another.

Did I mention Lisa's a good shot?

I glanced around for more 'converts.'

What I saw froze my heart.

About a dozen soldiers had been converted. It seemed too quick for that, but there they were, helping the twenty vamps drag my partner, too limp and way too pale, into the cave.

They had Patty.

A flash of movement made me turn to my right. I reached up and grabbed Wattson's collar as he ran past me.

"You can't help her in there, Al."

My voice sounded more in control than I felt.

"Time to go, Captain Martin."

Sam's squeaky voice echoed along the mountains, a bizarre sound in the middle of battle if there ever was one.

I looked for the little red head and soon found her, directing a half dozen soldiers as they put one of those vamps into a HUMVEE.

The back of the vehicle was a cage.

Metal bars.

Two inches thick.

Now I knew what our plan had been.

Damn.

"We need you to find out how to deal with these… things. That's how you'll help Patty."

I thought I sounded pretty optimistic.

But I didn't like the idea.

Not one bit.

Wattson's eyes told me he didn't either.

6

We had to get The Count back to the States for testing. I named it that on the drive back to the base.

Another long flight gave me a chance to test something. I leaned back into the seat, thought about Patty, and closed my eyes…

She was on her back, lying on a flat stone table, gold shackles on her hands and feet. They'd stripped her clothing, her torn skin now a lifeless grey. The stubs of her wings twitched in pools of blood.

There were a lot of the vamps there, maybe forty. All lined up by her feet.

Behind them, those other things grinned.

Excited.

DAMN!!

"Can you see anything? Can you see Patty? Is she all right?"

Wattson leaned over me, eager for anything to grasp onto. I could hear him adjusting his gizmo's dials.

If I'd said anything now, he'd read it in my voice.

So I just shook my head.

I reached up and knocked his gizmo out of his hands.

It deflated him. He plopped down in the seat next to Lisa, leaned forward and put his head in his hands.

"I'd never thought about girls, women. They never thought about me. Too much of a nerd. It was always 'study this' and 'discover that.' But Patty. She asked about *me*, she cared about *ME*, she… she liked me…"

Lisa did her best, stroking his shoulder, telling him that Patty would be okay. She was more convincing than I would have been.

Then again, she hadn't seen Patty, being mutilated and raped by monsters.

Being on the NYPD, you'd think you'd get used to things like that.

Cruelty.

Evil.

You don't.

At least, I didn't.

"Thank God."

It startled me that I said it out loud.

Wattson looked up at me, that ember of hope flickering into life.

I needed to keep that alive.

"She's alive. She's hurt, but she's alive."

Can angels be killed?

I didn't want to find out.

I knew Lisa would make me.

Wattson gushed a 'thank you' and went back to the sleeper area. I saw him kneeling next to a cot for a few minutes before he crawled in.

"John, what…"

"No. Just take what I told him." I nodded towards Wattson's cot, then I looked into Lisa's eyes.

"No. Anything else."

She swallowed a sob and kissed my forehead before she folded herself against me.

It's hard, not sleeping.

I knew if I had slept, they'd play games in my head. I needed to control that.

We flew.

We landed.

The Count was off-loaded in his cage.

More white HUMVEEs.

Sam driving too fast.

Soon enough we were in the bunker again.

Wattson and Lisa went to the lab to set up the testing regimen. Sam slapped my back.

"So, Captain Martin, I take it they are treating her very badly."

I looked down at her.

She had her eyes closed.

After several seconds she opened them.

A tear rolled down her cheek.

I nodded.

"Information will be the key to this, you know. Information we get from The Count, in there, and from…"

"Yeah. I know."

"Did you ever consider why you have this gift, Captain?"

"I, well, yeah. But I never could figure that out. Why me?"

"Have you considered that if you were eager to look at such things, you would not have been given this gift?"

I just looked at Sam.

She walked away, leaving me standing in the corridor outside my quarters.

Lisa and Wattson had gone to the lab. I had an idea Wattson wouldn't be overly gentle in his research on The Count. And I know what Lisa is like with a slow burn under her skin.

I felt sorry for the person The Count used to be.

I didn't feel sorry for the thing he was now.

Not one bit.

I don't remember opening the door or getting undressed.

Sam's words kept running through my mind.

I could see Patty. I could see what they did to her. I could see each one take his turn, looking straight at me, grunting and grinning at ME.

I could see Patty's perfect face, distorted with pain, with sadness. As each new monster continued her scourge, I could hear her perfect voice.

"I forgive you."

Then she turned her head and looked right at me.

She batted her eyes…

Every detective has a look, a signal they share with their partner. When Patty batted her eyes that way, she was telling me she needed help.

Damn.

I didn't know what to do.

As I watched, she stood up.

Well, she sort of stood up.

Part of her did.

Transparent.

Ghostly.

With wings.

Perfect.

She reached out and stroked my cheek.

"I'll survive. But just a little longer. Hurry."

"Wattson…"

She seemed to perk up at his name.

BZzzzzzzzzz…

Did I mention I hate alarm clocks?

I stood up and stretched, dropped my shorts and stepped into the shower. Under the hot water, I felt a little better. Not about Patty, but about why I see such things.

But I needed a plan to get her out of there.

Soon.

Somewhere between the shampoo and conditioner a pair of soapy hands ran up my back, over my shoulders and around my chest.

I felt the rest of her press into my back.

Something about Lisa always makes me feel like I can take on the whole world.

Right now, I needed that.

"There's a strategy meeting in twenty minutes. Sam wants you there."

We were ten minutes late.

"The coffee is in the back. Help yourselves." Sam squeaked. "Just be quick about it."

I got one for each of us and followed Lisa to the two open seats. After we sat, I took a sip and burned my tongue.

I'll never understand why the only options for serving coffee seem to be just under a boil or just above freezing.

"Captain Martin, will you please give us a summation of Miss O'Rourke's situation?"

"Patty is being held in the caverns in Turkey. She's hanging on, but I…" Lisa squeezed my arm, "we have to get her out of there soon."

"The good news is that the demons are pre-occupied with her. There have been no attacks reported since her capture." Sam didn't sound too happy to be telling us the 'good news.'

I shot a glance at Wattson. I expected him to be knotted up with worry.

He wasn't.

His jaw was clenched, his eyes clear and focused.

He was pissed.

But he was in control.

Good.

"How do we attack, is there a way to hurt them? What do you have for us, Professor?"

"Sam, our weapons give them pain, but haven't shown that they can really hurt these demons unless we blow them to bits. The only thing we've seen that really stops them is an attack by the Rods.

"Given the way the Rods attack, and what Dr. Martin and I have found out from the recovered pieces of the demon and from disec… examining our captive, I know we can hurt them, and I think I know how we can kill them."

"Continue, Professor."

"Their tissue is nearly indestructible in amounts over about a half pound. It can repair itself almost instantly. We'll have to chop them up into little pieces. Then we can burn them to death, with fire, extreme cold, chemicals, lye or acids."

"White phosphorus."

"Major?"

"White phosphorus. It ignites on exposure to air with a fire that can't be extinguished. When it's done burning, the residue is phosphoric acid. We have it in stock in grenades, mortar rounds, rockets, and artillery shells, and incendiary rounds of 7.62mm, .50cal, and 20mm size."

"Yes, that would seem to fit our needs, Major." The Major seemed pleased with Sam's confirmation.

"Excuse me, Professor, you mentioned extreme cold also. How do you burn something with extreme cold?" I don't like being confused.

"The effects of extreme cold on living tissue is much the same as that of extreme heat. Exposing the tissue to liquid nitrogen, or liquid oxygen, for several seconds will explode the cells, destroying their structure. Exposure to a powerful acid, such as hydrochloric or sulfuric, or to a powerful base, such as lye, will have a similar effect. The Rods digest them. Standard stomach acid."

92

"So, we have the means to destroy them if we can chop them up small enough?"

"Yes, Director. A flamethrower would work. We just need a way to chop them up, or burn them all at once. Any ideas?" Wattson looked over at the Marine Major sitting next to Sam.

"An explosive inside could work, but you'd likely end up with a bigger piece than a half pound. The thing would just grow back. Can you immobilize them, Professor?"

"That's the other part of our, eh, research. It sounds, well, superstitious, but it worked. Garlic."

"What?" everyone in the room echoed the word.

"Garlic introduced into their systems will paralyze them, at least the vampire form. It can be injected, ingested or aerosolized and inhaled."

"Injected. We have ordinance that can carry a substance into the bloodstream. How much is needed?"

"Rapid paralysis occurs with a 20mg per kilo dose. For the average sized vampire, about 70 kilos, that would be 1400mg. About a gram and a half, the size of one garlic clove."

"About one .50cal round, three 7.62mm rounds, or twenty to thirty 5.52mm rounds. We have the empty delivery ordinance in stock. Professor, can you get the garlic into a liquid form?"

"Very easily."

"I'll have a production station opened on the floor below your lab, Professor. Give me a list of what you need." Sam turned her attention to the Marine next to her. "Major, where do you need the liquid?"

"I'll have the men begin loading the ammo in the mess hall on D deck. Send it there."

Sam looked around the room. "Everyone, get busy. Major, Captain, with me please."

As we walked, the Major pulled out what looked like a cross between Captain Kirk's communicator and a cell phone. I found out later it was the modern version of a walkie-talkie. He gave instructions like he was ordering dinner. We ended up in Sam's briefing room.

"Please, sit down, gentlemen," she motioned to the padded chairs around a half-moon shaped table.

"Captain Martin, what can you tell us of their capabilities? What are their numbers, of the gargoyle types, the vampire types? Are there any other types we've yet to encounter?"

I sat back and closed my eyes.

Patty was alone now. She gave me a direction. I found the room.

Twelve of the demons sat around a table of sorts. There was one empty chair. Four of the demons were very thin, their skin a pale grey. They had a small mouth with only two teeth. Seven were the red kind I had seen at the school. The last demon was bigger than the rest. Much bigger. The other eleven seemed afraid of the big one.

And the big one looked pissed.

In the background, the vamps milled about, keeping a fair distance from the table. I guessed there were thirty or so there. I thought about it, and my view changed, flashing through the caverns and passages to the entrance.

I counted as I went.

Six hundred and sixty-six vampires.

Damn.

Back to the table. Something was going on, some type of planning. One of the smaller

94

demons made a motion, and the big cheese backhanded him across the face.

Hard.

It was like watching a movie of Hitler and his generals, planning the invasion of Russia, the maniac convinced he was invincible, and his generals too fearful to disagree.

Finally I saw the big one's claw hit down on the table. A map! I found I could change the angle to get a better view with a little concentration.

"Jerusalem. They will attack Jerusalem in two days."

"Damn!" Sam and the Major echoed my thoughts.

"That place is a powder keg now. Moving a big enough force in there to counter them could set off World War Three!"

"You are right, Major. So, we do *not* attack with brute force. We need a more…subtle approach. Captain Martin?"

"Major, don't those really big bombs work by aerosolizing a liquid explosive?"

"The MOABs. Yes. Good thinking, Captain! We fill one up with Wattson's garlic juice, and drop it on the cavern openings as these things come out. Closer in, we use white phosphorus mortars and grenades. Then it's a matter of feeding what's left through the chippers."

"Chippers?"

"Wood chippers. One hundred and twenty heavy duty wood chippers, each one set to empty the remains into a large vat of liquid oxygen."

"Why not liquid nitrogen, or acid?"

"Liquid nitrogen is too cold, it makes the containers too brittle and it evaporates too fast. It won't last long enough. And, it's

95

hard to get the required quantities. Acids and bases strong enough to do the job present environmental and handling issues. LOX is common, stable enough to be effective, and readily available in the required quantities."

"We seem to have a workable plan, gentlemen. To your tasks then, Major. Captain Martin, well done. Dinner is on me tonight. Bring your wife."

Damn.

Lisa insisted we dress for dinner. I don't know where she got that green dress.

Did I mention that green is my favorite color?

I made her put it on three times.

I had two years to make up for.

All I had was my usual detective's uniform, a charcoal grey suit, white shirt, black necktie. It worked. The two years of bloodstains had pretty much faded.

Dinner went pretty well, for a while. Sam was a gracious hostess, and the briefing room made a passable dining room.

The conversation was good enough.

The food was decent, too.

"So, Captain Martin, how did you end up in the City of New York Police Department?"

"I was a young kid, looking to make a difference in the world. It seemed like the place to do that."

"And Mrs. Martin, how did you meet her?"

A glance at Lisa confirmed what I already knew; she'd blushed and rolled her eyes.

"Murder. At Columbia. She was pre-med. I showed up and started asking questions; 'Did you see anything. Did you hear anything. Do you have a boyfriend.' She kept saying 'no.' Two years later she said 'yes.' Ten years after that…"

"What John means to say is, we had some hard times. I took the M.E. job to stay close to him. I was too close sometimes. Not close enough other times. The hours didn't mesh. But mostly the things we saw, they…they wore on us. On me." Lisa turned from Sam and looked at me.

She swallowed. "I think it's time we tried 'us' again."

I'd forgotten that little hand squeeze, the one under the table. The one that says, 'I'm yours. You're mine.'

"Now it's your turn, Sam. How did you become the top SISSI?"

"Your humor is obvious but amusing, Captain. I also wanted to change the world. I'd seen more than my share of bullies growing up. I joined the one organization where I would be helping to keep the worst of them in check. The ultimate anti-bullies."

"You joined the Marine Corps."

"Very good. Yes, I became a Marine."

"But your size? Aren't you shorter than the requirements?"

A glass of wine still relaxed Lisa's inhibitions.

"Yes, Mrs. Martin. However, one soon learns that nearly everything in life is negotiable, that every hard and steadfast rule has its exception. Let's just say I convinced them to make an exception. I spent twenty four years in the USMC before I was asked to join SISSI. That was thirty five years ago. Ten years ago, I became the Director."

"But, that would make you…" Lisa was halfway through her second glass of wine.

I didn't need to count.

"Yes, I am older than every living

President. Now, what do we do with you, Dr. Martin, when your husband goes to Jerusalem?"

"What do you mean, 'What do we do with me?' I'm going too."

"You're too valuable. I can't risk you. I can't risk Big Boy here getting cut in half because he's looking for you."

"I…" Lisa started to stand up, then plopped back down. She sat quietly for too long a time.

"I won't be distracted." It was a lame defense, but it was all I had. And, it wasn't true.

Sam dropped her chin and peered at me.

"I'm going where he goes. I don't care if it's into the bowels of Hell. I will not be apart from him again. You will not keep me from him."

I'd never heard this voice from Lisa.

Quiet.

Powerful.

Scary.

Damn.

Sam looked at Lisa, squinting as if the sun was behind her.

"You are quite sure of this, Mrs. Martin?"

The waiter leaned over Sam just then. I thought his hand looked pale, so I looked at his face. I saw a glint of light reflected from his long, needle-like teeth…

The three slugs from the 45 didn't kill the thing, but they did drive it back. I was over the table and on top of it pretty quickly, grabbing two steak knives as I went.

I slammed a knife down into each of its wrists, pinning it to the floor.

It snapped its jaws at me.

Now I just had to figure out my next move…

Lisa did that for me.

"John! Stand clear!"

She had a bucket of something, and when I stood up she doused the vamp with it. The thing began to smoke.

And scream.

And melt.

In a flash, Lisa had another bucket full and tossed it over the vamp again.

It took a long time for the thing to dissolve. Lisa poured a third bucket on the thing, and that did it.

By then I could barely breath.

The carpet was gone for about six feet around the thing.

"Good grief, Lisa, what was that stuff?"

"Hydrochloric acid. Good thing there's a supply of cleaning goods in your kitchen, Sam."

"You dumped the bleach and ammonia into the bucket. Quick thinking, Dr. Martin. And, welcome to our team."

By then the Major, a half dozen Marines, and Wattson were in the room.

"How much bleach and ammonia did she have in there?"

"Enough. Too much. Director Marlowe, just one thing. I was wondering why the director of SISSI would have three gallons each of bleach and ammonia in her kitchen?"

"Dr. Martin, let's just put it down to a woman's intuition."

I stared at her as Sam walked away.

Then she stopped, looked down at the smoldering hole in her carpet, and turned around.

"Captain Martin. Would you please explain how you were able to thrust two Sterling silver steak knives through the creature's wrists and four inches deep into the concrete floor?"

"I work out."

"I see."

Sam half smiled, nodded, and walked away.

Lisa grabbed my arm. I looked down at those eyes, staring up with that 'You're my knight in shining armor' look.

I knew she'd done a lot of the quick thinking and fast action with the acid and all, but I still felt twenty feet tall when she looked at me like that.

I hoped I always would.

"You were amazing!"

"Uh, well…yeah, uh…I, um…."

Who the hell set the clock to Junior High?

She kissed me.

Hard.

I closed my eyes.

I saw Patty.

Damn.

I took a step back. Lisa looked hurt for a second, then she looked worried.

"Patty."

"Yeah." My voice sounded like boulders eating gravel.

She hadn't been moved from that table. She was alone, but she looked…

Worse.

Pale.

Drained.

Dying.

"DAMN!"

Lisa wrapped her arms around me.

It helped.

Me

And Patty.

A little.

Something caught fire deep inside me.

Smoldering.

My partner.

I'd lost one partner to this case.

Not another.

"Lord, please protect her until I can…"

Lisa stepped back, looking up, worried…

Her silver cross glistened on her neck.

"John, be smart."

"That's why you're with me."

I kissed her forehead, pulled her close.

I rested my chin on the top of her head.

I could think that way.

The demons and vamps were feeling good right now. I could feel it.

They'd come out soon, trying to spread their terror, fear, hopelessness, and despair.

They fed off of those.

"There has to be a way to use that."

"Set a trap."

Lisa and I both looked up at Wattson.

My eyes grew wide.

Lisa gasped.

His face was…

Mean.

"We set a trap, like for any predator. Choice prey in easy reach."

He gulped.

Twice.

"Kids. Out in the open, near the caves."

"Al, you don't mean…"

"Oh, we'll be ready. The kids should…will be safe. I'll have them waiting."

"Them?"

Lisa's voice sounded good in chorus with mine.

"The Rods. I think I can call them. I know how now."

"Please, Professor Wattson, elaborate."

I hadn't heard Sam return. Her squeaky voice startled me.

"They come to protect good and destroy Evil. I know what they focus on. I can reproduce it."

"You have a 'Rod caller?' Can you be sure it works?"

Sam sounded skeptical.

"Reasonably sure. But, to test it may tip off our hand."

They flashed in front of my eyes, arguing.

Passionate.

Angry.

"They already know. About the Rods. Like fish know of Herron. We need another plan."

Everyone looked at me, as if I would have all the answers at my fingertips.

I didn't know what to say.

I panicked.

Something kicked in. Something from my childhood…

Please, God, help me do the right thing!

I saw Patty.

Stronger.

Smiling.

It came to me then.

"They are expecting a trap. We give them one, with the Marines as the obvious jaws, not the Rods. They'll come ready for Marines."

"Then we hit them with the Rods. Good, captain Martin!"

Sam sounded genuinely pleased.

Something told me it could work…

If…

102

7

They weren't kids.

Not really.

Just young.

Seventeen, eighteen.

Raw recruits.

Pre-boot camp.

Pre-Marines.

Okay, they were kids.

We had to get the things out in the open, so I could move in behind them to go get Patty.

That was the plan.

It sucked.

We all knew it, but we didn't have anything better.

We put the kids on an archeological dig site, about a mile from the cavern entrance.

I felt like crap for doing it.

The kids knew.

They had all volunteered.

Wattson was sure the Rods would win the day.

It took the monsters two hours to size things up and come out to… play.

They sent the vamps out first.

The Marines hit them.

Hard.

They had silver bullets.

Wattson and Lisa hadn't thought of that angle. Silver bullets were for Werewolves, after all.

The steak knives gave us the clue. Wattson verified it.

Seems silver works better than garlic.

Three or four well-placed rounds stopped

them cold.

An airburst mortar round of white phosphorus burned what was left.

A couple hundred of the vamps melted before the demons came out.

They were pissed.

Silver bullets only made them madder.

Like they needed to be madder.

My job was to sneak in behind them if the opportunity presented itself.

Lisa was coming with me.

I remember telling myself that wasn't so bad, that we were a damn good team.

I didn't buy it.

I worried.

It almost got her killed.

We ran into the cave after the eleventh demon came out. I knew the Marines were getting Hell, but that was their job in this.

Into the darkness, and down we ran.

Down.

Down.

Did I mention it was a long ways down?

The cavern split several times.

It seemed like we ran for an hour.

We rounded a corner, and saw some light…

And ran into ten angry demons returning to the cavern.

I don't know how we survived.

I know I woke up.

Sore and battered.

And alone.

DAMN!

DAMN!

DAMN!

Sam was there.

And Wattson.

104

And the Major.

Lisa wasn't.

I thought I was going to explode.

"Captain Martin, try to stay calm."

"Easy for you to say. Half of you isn't…"

"Half of me died bringing you here," Her voice cracked. "…on that train."

I looked at her.

Sam had a tear in her eye.

"Freddie."

"Yes. Now, we must get back to work."

She turned and climbed into the HUMVEE. I followed.

Numb.

"Hang on. I drive faster when I'm pissed."

Damn.

I survived the trip back to our base.

And the flight back to the bunker.

Barely.

I didn't sleep.

I didn't blink.

I didn't want to see what they were doing to Lisa.

I held out for two days.

I could feel my eyes closing.

I couldn't stop them.

Damn.

She was sitting in a chair.

Still with the same khakis on.

Looking bored.

She was next to Patty.

Patty looked…

Better.

The demons looked pissed.

Every so often one would move towards Lisa and Patty.

It was like they hit a stonewall.

"They will not harm her as long as you are alive"

Still, I wanted them out of there.

NOW.

The briefing was…

Brief.

"Captain Martin, to bring you up to speed; we lost three of the recruits, and thirty seven Marines. We managed to destroy all three hundred of the vamps they sent out, and one of the demons as well."

"They took her."

"Yes, they did."

"I need her."

"Yes, you do."

I stared at Sam for about an hour.

It was four seconds.

"The Rods didn't come."

"No, they didn't. That being said, we did better against them than we expected."

I glared at the Major, then at Wattson.

"Why?"

"I don't know. I sent the signals that should have called them. They didn't come."

"Where were they? Where did you send the signals?"

"The nearest hive was in Naples. They should have come from all over the Earth… Oh, my God! I sent the signals too late!"

"Their cavern isn't a physical location. It shifts and moves. We need to go to New York."

I just knew.

"Captain Martin, what are you saying?"

"I'm saying we need to get our sorry-assed group to Yonkers if we're going to win this. Wattson, call the Rods, try and get them to follow us there."

"I think I understand. A trans-dimensional shifting…"

"The explanation doesn't matter! Just bring them!"

I turned and stomped out of the briefing room.

I needed to sleep.

Or pound on something.

I smiled when I first saw him. Then I remembered.

I remembered the beating he gave me.

I remembered the hole blown in his chest.

I sat up.

"Whoa, partner. Relax."

Po's voice could stroke you like velvet gloves at times.

"What, why, how…"

"You're dreaming. It's easier that way."

"Po, I'm sorr…"

"It's me who should apologize. I blamed you for what that monster did to Cleo. That was wrong. I'm sorry, John."

"Po, I…"

"We need to get Lisa and your partner out of there. Soon."

"I'm all ears."

"They'll come for you, John. You, Patty, and Lisa are the key. They need to get you three out of the way to win. They need you dead. Then they go after everything else."

"So, I'm the bait."

"Looks like it, partner."

"Po, can you…"

"No. This is about all I can do in this, John. You'll need to rely on those around you. You're not alone."

I swallowed hard. I think it was Kansas.

"Look for the cave where those kids were. With the cougar. That's a good place to start…"

Everything faded out then.

I sat up.

I got out of bed.

I showered.

The stall still smelled like Jasmine.

Like her.

I leaned on the wall for a long time, the water running down my back.

I waited, but Lisa didn't come into the shower.

I pounded the wall a couple of times.

Damn.

When I got dressed I went to Sam's quarters.

The door opened before I could knock.

"Captain Martin. Good. Come in."

We hatched the plan.

Together.

Too bad it didn't work.

I was supposed to sneak in behind them again. This time with a geo-magnetic GPS gizmo-thingy that would keep me from going in circles, even if I were underground.

Instead, the demons came out and killed everything.

And everyone.

Except me.

The Marines got it first.

The demons flew out of the cave and went up.

They came down behind everyone.

In the town.

Each demon dropped thirteen vamps into the town.

The Marines double-timed it, trying to

save the town.

The demons ate them.

All.

Then they came after us.

I snuck into the cave, but only after I saw the Marines, the Major, and Sam cut in half.

Wattson's Rods were late again.

Damn.

So here I am, trying to figure out if the plan will still work.

I'm walking through the caverns now, eyes closed.

The GPS thing died an hour ago.

I think Lisa and Patty are just ahead.

I know those things are following me.

Every ten yards or so I drop a grenade.

Silver frags and a white phosphorus core.

I heard them scream every time one went off.

A wider area here. I dropped the last four grenades.

The ones rigged with the remote detonator.

Just a little more.

"John, you know it will help. Do it."

"Po, I..."

I took a big breath.

"Yea, though I walk through the Valley of the Shadow Death, I fear no evil..."

I kept reciting the Psalm.

I felt it hurt them.

Almost there...

Around a corner, and there they were.

My angels.

I tossed the detonator to Lisa, along with the silver-plated Bowie knife.

"John! NO!"

I turned and ran at the things.
They were farther away than I thought.
I was getting winded quick.
Maybe running wasn't the best plan.
Did I mention that I hate running?
Then they were there.
Ten of them.
Nine were thirty feet long.
The tenth was…
Bigger.
This time I had a bigger sword.
I swung it.
Hard.
The closest demon lost his head.
Claws reached out for me.
Something blocked the blow.
I swung the silver-plated sword again.
Another lost its head.
I was beginning to get optimistic.
Jaws snapped at me.
Again something powerful deflected them.
Then they came at me.
All at once.
Together.
Po couldn't stop them all.
"Lord, let me last long enough for them to reach safety."
A demon's fist hit my head.
I fell.
They came over me.
The closest demon opened his mouth.
It smelled awful!
The jaws began to close.
Then it…
Vanished.
A bite at a time.

110

I could see the ripples.

Everywhere.

There must have been ten thousand of them, swirling around the demons, eating them.

I got up and swung the sword again.

My arms ached.

Broad swords are heavy!

"Thy Rod…"

I swung again…

"…and Thy Staff,"

I swung once more…

"…they comfort me…"

I could barely hold the sword now. The tip fell to the floor of the cave as I watched the air ripple around the tenth demon. Chunks of him vanished.

The big one opened that putrid mouth and bit the ripples.

Three bites and the Rods were gone.

All of them.

Most of the tenth demon was gone too.

I took a step back.

"*JOHN!*"

"LISA! NOW!"

The grenades knocked the demon over just as his huge fist slammed into my chest. I couldn't breathe, but somehow I got to my feet.

The thing's tail was gone.

It seemed…

Angrier.

"The two. They are MY toys. Join with me, to rule this place, and I will share them with you. Them, and all else you desire…"

"Go to…" Somewhere I found the strength to lift the tip of the sword…

"HELL!"

Mac's voice finished my sentence before

the explosions drowned her out.

At least three rocket grenades punched into the thing's guts.

The explosions ripped it apart.

The whole Precinct was there.

And more.

A lot more.

Wattson was there, sword in hand.

He'd brought Mac.

Mac brought half the NYPD.

"Mac! You look damn good!"

"Martin, where in hell is your partner?"

Epilogue

They never asked me, really.

They just showed me where my office was.

At least they fixed the carpet.

Mac was fit to be tied, but made sure I knew that Patty and I were only 'on loan.'

There was a cheap plastic nameplate in the desk.

I left it there.

It was Marlowe's desk after all.

I was just on loan.

The living quarters in the bunker aren't bad.

Lisa fixed ours up.

I managed to convince Wattson to stay on in research.

Well, Patty did.

The Vice President stopped by. He said thanks and such, then welcomed me.

The new Director of SISSI.

Go figure.

Damn!

About James W. McAllister

I am a Registered Respiratory
Therapist living near Syracuse in
Central New York State. Currently I am
employed in Healthcare Accreditation.

I founded Fortiter Publishing LLC in
November 2013 as a vehicle to get all
these great Science Fiction and Fantasy
stories out of my head. "FORTITER" is
inscribed on the MacAlister Clan Crest.
The word means "to go forward, boldly."
I am grateful for the Clan Chief's
permission to use the Crest and Tartan
in my company's logo, and to use
"FORTITER" in my company's name.

I have been interested in science
fiction since reading the Lensmen Series
of books by E. E. "Doc" Smith in Junior
High School.

See my Amazon Author's page here:
http://amazon.com/author/jwmcallister

I hope you enjoyed my story. If you
did, please leave a review.